# The Yellow Note

April Ann Roy

Copyright © 2008 by April Ann Roy

*The Yellow Note*
by April Ann Roy

Printed in the United States of America

ISBN 978-1-60791-038-1

All rights reserved solely by the author. The author guarantees all contents are original and do not infringe upon the legal rights of any other person or work. No part of this book may be reproduced in any form without the permission of the author. The views expressed in this book are not necessarily those of the publisher.

www.xulonpress.com

This novel is a work of fiction. Names, characters, places and incidents are either the product of the author's imagination or are used fictitiously. Any resemblance to actual events, locales, organizations or persons, living or dead, is entirely coincidental and beyond the intent of the author.

# ACKNOWLEDGEMENTS

First and foremost, all honor goes to my Lord and Savior Jesus Christ who gave me the gift to write, I appreciate the gift very much. Without You I am nothing, but with You, I can do all things! And You took me through all these years, teaching me, guiding me, and helping me understand writing better. I know there is so much more to learn, but I know you'll be with me every step.

To Sherri, my aunt, who took the time to edit my book for me. You know, all those hundreds of books you read wasn't just for you. Thanks so much for being my second set of eyes and for using the red pen to mark away!

And to my husband Jason, my partner for life. You pushed me and encouraged me and now I'm doing something I never thought I'd really do. I'm publishing my first book!!! You've helped me see the potential inside me and gave me a positive outlook even when I thought I sucked.

# CHAPTER ONE

### *HYPOCRITES DESERVE DEATH*

Laura Thayer stared down at the little yellow note. It was just like the others. Writen in the same style, on the same paper and with the same black marker.

Hypocrites deserve death? She scowled, her face getting hot and red.

Laura stood next to her locker, thinking and rethinking, holding the paper in her sweaty palms. How did it get taped to the inside of her locker anyway? Only James, her boyfriend, knew the combination, at least she thought so. She hadn't given it to anyone else, not even her closest friends.

Whatever.

She grabbed her geometry book, checked her make-up in the little magnet mirror she'd hung in the locker. Laura groaned seeing a little red zit appearing on her forehead. She couldn't do anything about it now, she'd be late. She slammed the locker shut. As she waltzed down the hall, head high, swaying

*The Yellow Note*

her hips in her freshly cleaned cheerleading outfit, she saw the goth girls. That's what the kid's at Raile High School called them. Freaks, weirdoes, outcasts, whatever derogatory name came to mind.

Laura hated them both. They were a detriment to her popularity and they caused problems. She couldn't stand the way they dressed, all in black, drab clothing, dark make-up and pasty pale like a ghost...they avoided the sun like the plague.

Both of them were standing at the end of the hall near the garbage can. They might as well just crawl inside, because that's where they belonged. Laura wondered if one of them had been sending her the little yellow notes. It would be just like them, calling her evil names, trying to scare her. Laura's anger grew. They were all sinners. All going to hell. She hated them. How dare they even look at her! She was the Christian, the righteous one, they should all bow in her presence.

Laura veered across the hallway through the crowd of bodies and made her way to where they stood. She stopped in front of them, looked them in the eye and then crumpled the note slowly, purposefully, showing them she wasn't scared. Then she dropped the wad into the trash can and walked away, but not without bumping into Chloe. The girl pushed her back really hard, almost knocking Laura to the floor. Laura just straightened herself and kept walking, smiling at the students who passed her. This was *her* school, no one could make her do anything.

*The Yellow Note*

"I think his mom hits him." Steven said.

Pete Monson watched his fifteen year old son shovel food into his mouth as he spoke, like he hadn't eaten for weeks. Must be a growing thing, although he couldn't remember eating that much at Steve's age. *The kid could use some weight,* Pete thought as he tried to finish his own food. Steve was almost as tall as Pete now, but he was lanky with big feet and long narrow hands. Pete tried to remember if he'd looked like that at Steve's age.

"It's the second time I've seen him with a bruise on his face since school started." Steve continued. A dribble of spaghetti sauce ran down his chin and he wiped it with the back of his hand, then onto the thigh of his new jeans. Pete cringed and glanced as his wife Kristine.

"Steven!" Kristine shouted. Her bluish gray eyes shot spears at the boy. Steve jerked because of her sudden outburst and his face turned red.

"Sorry." Steve looked down at his jeans.

"I just bought those pants last week." Kristine went on. Steve nodded and dabbed his pants with a napkin.

"Why do you think she hits him?" Pete asked. He wanted to stop Kristine from the nagging that usually continued until the situation was run raw.

"Both times Zack had some dumb excuse about getting hit with a basketball during practice or something." Steve horsed down the last bite of his spaghetti. Pete looked down at his plate of food, half eaten and getting cold. He wasn't really hungry

*The Yellow Note*

tonight. "I've never seen him get hit in practice. At least not hard enough for a bruise."

"Hmm." Pete nodded. He wasn't that interested. Steve was probably making something out of nothing. Pete pushed his soggy noodles around on the intricately designed dinner plate, his attention elsewhere. His daughter Heather. She hadn't come home for dinner and no one had said anything about it. It wasn't unusual, but it didn't stop him from wondering either. He was always wondering.

Pete could hear Steve rambling on about Zack and his mother and all the details about it. He didn't retain a word of it, just kept nodding at the right time and when there was a long pause. Pete guessed he was finished.

"I'm sure everything will be fine." Pete said.

Steve and Kristine both stared at him blankly. Maybe he'd missed something. He looked from his wife to his son and then back to his plate. Now he felt stupid. He should have been paying attention.

"Can I be excused please?" Steve asked his mom for the okay. Pete shook his head and rolled his eyes, he never cared when anyone left the table. What did it matter if the kid didn't ask to leave? He was finished with dinner, there was nothing else to do at the dinning room table except stare at each other in awkward silence.

"Sure, Steven." Kristine nodded at him. He got up and left the dining room and Kristine kept on eating in her dainty manner, her long slender fingers grasping her fork just so. Right now it bugged Pete. Everything had to be just right with her, from her

*The Yellow Note*

clothing and make-up to the entire ensemble of their house.

"What?" She asked, finally realizing he was staring at her.

"Nothing." Pete focused on his food again.

"You were going to make a comment about table manners, weren't you?" She put her fork on her empty plate and looked at him, her eyes testing him. When he didn't answer she stood up in a huff and took all three plates from the table to the kitchen. Pete sighed.

He got up from the table as well, straightened the chairs and picked up all the dirty napkins. Steve's place across from him and Kristine was a disaster. There were crumbs everywhere from the garlic bread and a few drips of red sauce on the elegant table cloth. "Great." Pete mumbled, knowing what would come of that sight. He was actually surprised Kristine didn't see it when she picked up the plates.

He tried to rub it off but it only made the spots worse. The cream colored fabric would have to be cleaned. Something Kristine would sigh about. She would complain that she had to many things to do, that the table cloth was just another addition to her pile. And Pete would wonder why she was even fretting because they had a house keeper who came in a few times a week while everyone was at work or school to do the things Kristine didn't have time for anymore.

So, to avoid the turmoil for a little while longer, Pete pulled the silk center piece a few inches towards Steve's place. Perfect. It covered the two spots. The

*The Yellow Note*

only thing was that the mid-table decoration was now off just a tad. No one else would really notice it, except Kristine. Pete knew his efforts were in vain.

Kristine came back from the kitchen and Pete stood upright quickly. She grabbed the linen napkins and then looked down at the table. She frowned and began to straighten the center runner. Pete groaned inside. He began to move towards the kitchen door with the salt and pepper shakers in hand.

"What on earth!" Kristine gasped. She bent over the table, staring at Steve's area. "Did he cover this so I wouldn't see it?" She touched the little red spots.

"No, I did." Pete said. He stopped.

"What? Why?" She stood up, hands on her hips, head cocked, and looked at him like he was some kind of weirdo.

"Because I knew you'd flip out." Oh, no. He'd just said that, right? It wasn't just a thought. Pete took a deep breath, preparing himself for whatever might come. He really wished he would have gotten up with Steve and just left the table. At least then Steve would be the only one who would answer for the spilled spaghetti sauce. Now it would be both their heads and all Pete was trying to do, was give the kid some slack!

"Oh, I see." Kristine crossed her arms tight over her black suit coat. She narrowed her eyes at him. He was glad the long table was between them.
"So, I'm the bad guy here. I try to keep this house as nice as possible. We have guests from time to time you know, important clients of mine, friends of ours, people from church...respectable people."

*The Yellow Note*

"I like a nice house too Kris, but sometimes you just go a little overboard, that's all I'm saying." Pete turned to the swinging door and entered the recently remodeled kitchen. The huge room had all the latest appliances, plenty of space on the granite counter tops and almost endless storage supply.

As Pete put the salt and pepper shakers away above the six burner gas range, he heard Kristine burst into the kitchen behind him. Her heels clicked loudly on the sand colored tile floor. She made it to the center island and put her hands down on it. It was obvious she was peeved.

"We have an image to uphold Pete. I know you know this, but what kind of people have stains on their linens and haphazardly placed things throughout the house?" She tapped her long fingernails on the counter. Pete could feel her eyes boring into his back. "People like that are lazy, incompetent and certainly not upstanding citizens. I'm sure God likes a clean house, so I intend to keep it that way."

Pete turned from the stove area to his wife. "I think you should lighten up a bit. Steve is still a kid. He just turned fifteen and school only started a few weeks ago. He's probably got a lot running through his head, I'm sure he didn't purposely get your freshly pressed table cloth dirty."

"And those jeans..." Kristine shook her head like she hadn't heard a word Pete had just said. She grabbed the butter off the island and put it into the wide, stainless steel refrigerator. "Those are Keshiel brand jeans. Very popular right now, and expensive."

*The Yellow Note*

Pete watched and listened to his wife rant about the jeans as she rinsed the dishes and put them in the dishwasher. After that she wiped the counters and started in on Heather and the clothing she chose to wear. *It may never end!* Pete clenched his jaw, the anger boiling inside of him. He couldn't stop it. He didn't want to.

"Shut up!" Pete finally yelled. Kristine jumped. She dropped the sponge front her hand and stared at him. "Don't you ever listen to yourself?" Pete flung his hands up. "No wonder Heather thinks that the only thing we care about is appearance! And I'm not even the one who cares. She lumps me in with you because we're the parents and she assumes that what you think, I think it too."

Kristine's mouth hung open. It took her a second to process what had just happened. Normally, Pete was so non-confrontational. He even surprised himself with this sudden onslaught of craziness. But it felt so good to let it out.

"I can't believe you just told me to shut up." Her lip trembled. For a second Pete felt bad for yelling, but when Kristine's eyes turned cold he lost that emotion. "You never talk to her." She pointed a finger at him.

"Neither do you. You nag her." Pete crossed his arms. This wasn't his fault, not this argument, not Heather's attitude, not anything.

"I don't nag, I correct, Pete. And I do it alone because you refuse to even acknowledge that our daughter has strayed from God and is running around

*The Yellow Note*

with the most horrid crowd of young people at the school."

"She's seventeen Kris, she's not perfect. And neither are you." For that one she glared at him.

"Just because Heather is 17 doesn't mean she can do whatever she pleases and get away with it. You never enforce rules around here so I'm left the dirty work. Which means I always look like the old hag who doesn't care about having fun." Kristine ripped the little plastic clip out of her soft, auburn hair. It fell out of the tight bun she'd had it in to her shoulders. She began to massage her scalp.

"Well, it's not *fun* around here!" Pete yelled again. He was almost liking this out of control feeling, letting his temper get the best of him. "All you do is complain about Heather and nag her about every little thing on the planet and then Steve, who does the best he can, gets picked at about these silly little details like asking to leave the table after meals! Holy cow Kris, live a little!"

Her face contorted, her breathing got heavy and her face turned the deepest shade of red Pete had ever seen. It was sort of funny.

"Live a little?" She mockingly chuckled. "It's my money that bought us this house, our cars and all the things we have. It's me who cleans the house and reprimands the kids and takes care of the bills. I'm the one who built my own company from scratch so we could live like this. You're the one who runs off and plays child games as an investigator at the police department all day long. I could live a little

*The Yellow Note*

if someone stepped up and became the man of the house."

Ouch!

Pete recoiled, unable to say a darn thing. Kristine spun around and exited the kitchen with her head high, obviously aware of how she'd hurt Pete and not seeming to care. And she wondered why he didn't want to be home much.

Pete zoned out in front of the television, flipping channels on the satellite. Nothing was on. He landed on the news and stayed there, half listening, half thinking. He was still festering with irritation, not sure what to do with it. He didn't have the energy to confront Kristine again. He never did. In fact, this was the first time in years that he'd ever let himself fly off the handle like he had. It was amazing it wasn't constant. Kristine was continually backing him into corners, pushing him to the limit and walking away with the last word.

Pete grit his teeth and slid deeper into the brushed leather sofa, wanting to pour his can of soda all over its beige surface. That was silly though. He'd be ruining his own thing, and he loved his sofa.

"Dad?" Steve's voice came from the wide doorway to the living room where he stood looking sheepish. Pete looked up.

"Yeah."

"I heard you and mom arguing." He came in and sat on the other end of the sofa from Pete.

*The Yellow Note*

"Sorry you had to hear it." Pete said. If anyone could calm him it was Steve. Even if he spilled at the dinner table or got grass stains on his clothing, he was the most considerate young man Pete knew. He always tried to sort things out, always watching, never saying a harsh word and constantly looking for ways to make things better. It was rare if he complained. Even when Heather was a real jerk to him, he kept his mouth shut.

"Did I ruin the tablecloth?" He asked.

"No." Pete smiled and shook his head. "Your mom just wants things nice. It's not your fault, it was an accident."

"Not my jeans though." Steve frowned. "I guess I wasn't even thinking because I was talking to you."

"It's okay. Don't worry about it. Mom's just tense or something." Pete turned to the television.

"Why?"

"I don't know." Pete shrugged. And he wasn't lying. He couldn't remember when, but somehow Kristine had changed. She'd always been a bit of a worry wart, but at the same time she'd been easy going, fun, looking for ways to change the routine. Now it was different.

"Why don't you talk to her about it?" Steve asked. Pete looked at him again. His face was sad.

"It's not that simple Steve."

"Talking is always simple, it's pride that makes it hard."

Pete didn't want to hear that, not from his son, not from anyone. He wasn't prideful. Kristine was

*The Yellow Note*

the one making it hard. She wouldn't even see his side of things.

"Did you finish your homework?" Pete asked. Pointless question really because Steve always did his homework, without being asked.

"Yeah." He stood up and walked to the living room door. "Good night dad."

"Night, Steve."

"And just for the record, I don't think being a detective is a waste of time. Money isn't everything." He grinned and left Pete alone in the dim room.

The TV flashed lights on the walls, blue, then green and white. Pete gazed out into the dark entry way by the front door. Right. Money wasn't everything. Kristine was caught up in all things that looked nice. Maybe that was her problem. Money. Pete certainly didn't care. Yeah, it was easy to be able to buy just about anything he wanted, go on vacation when they wanted—which they hadn't done for years—and not worry if the bills were going to be paid. But his dream was his job. Investigation. Helping people who needed it and wanted it. It didn't matter if he made six figures or not.

Stupid money.

Pete clicked the TV off and left the room, climbing the steps to their bedroom. The lights were off which meant that Kristine was probably asleep. Instead of waking her, which he wanted to do, he carefully found their bathroom and turned the light on in there. It illuminated the room enough to see what he was doing, and to see that Kristine was not in bed. Her pillow was gone. Pete turned back to the bathroom

*The Yellow Note*

and opened the mirror cabinet. Her toothbrush and a few other personal items were gone too.

He rolled his eyes and slammed the cabinet door shut. She was sleeping in the guest bedroom in the basement. Well, if she was going to be that childish, he could be too.


Pete was vaguely aware of some noise in the hallway, creaking floor or something. He lay in bed, trying to figure out what it was as he pulled his mind from dream land. Suddenly, a light flipped on at the other end near Heather's room.

"Did you think you could just sneak in?" Kristine's voice. Pete couldn't see from where he was. He'd have to get up and poke his head around the corner. He wasn't about to.

"I wasn't sneaking." Heather said. Pete looked at the digital clock next to his bed. It was after midnight.

"Where were you?"

"Chloe's house." Pete heard the sound of Heather's bedroom door opening.

"Doesn't her sister care that you're there so late?"

"No, she's not a crab like you."

There was a long pause. "Is that alcohol I smell?" Kristine demanded to know.

"Yep." Heather sighed.

"You're grounded from using your car. I'm taking your keys away."

"Fine, fetch."

*The Yellow Note*

Keys rattled and then hit the floor downstairs in the entry. Kristine gasped. Pete assumed Heather had thrown her keys over the hallways banister.

"Heather, it's for your own good. You could get your license taken away for driving drunk as a minor, or you could be killed."

"Not that you'd care." A door slammed. Kristine mumbled something and the light in the hall flipped off.

Pete changed his position. Kristine must have radar ears to hear Heather come in through the garage door. The downstairs guest bedroom was on the opposite end of the house. It was like she was waiting for Heather to do something wrong so that she could make a big deal about it.

Now Pete couldn't go back to sleep. He moved around so many times that finally he sat up in the darkness and looked around. The little light near the bathroom floor eased out onto the bedroom's tan carpet. Pete glanced at the clock again. It had been an hour since Heather came home. Seemed like three.

The clocks blue numbers shone on the night stand. Pete's watch sat there and under that his Bible. He stared at the gold words, HOLY BIBLE. He'd purchased it at their church. The Lord's Fellowship Church. Over 1,000 members and growing. The largest Christian church in the city of Raile. Kristine seemed proud to attend and that many people knew them there.

Pete reached for the Bible, his watch sliding off of it to the table. He just held it, his finger running over the indented gold letters in the black leather cover. Right now he felt too guilty to open the cover, too guilty to pray even. He lay back down with the Book on his chest and fell asleep.

# CHAPTER TWO

Don Graham smiled down at his 5-year-old yellow lab as she walked happily next to him. Her belly swayed back and forth with each step, her rich brown eyes were kind when she returned Don's smile. Brownie was her name. A childish name, Don knew, but it was as a child he'd had another yellow lab that he and his brother had named Brownie. Brownie number one died when she was just eight after having found some kind of poison in the garage.

Don swore he'd never own a dog again, losing such a friend had been hard. Especially, since Don had always been a loner. But five years ago he'd been taking his usual afternoon walk and saw a pen full of delightful blonde pups. The sign had said, 'Free to Good Home'. Accidental breeding. And even though it had been to another yellow lab, the owners didn't want dogs that didn't have a certified bloodline.

Instantly, Don had narrowed in on the little runt who played alone. It was as if they'd been meant for each other. So a half hour later the 8-week-old puppy

*The Yellow Note*

was in Don's arms being carried the ten blocks away to his house.

Don smiled wider thinking about it.

"Perfect day, isn't it girl." He said taking a deep breath and looking up at the vibrant blue sky. The normally sultry weather of Raile had blown away with a front, leaving behind lower temperatures and a reprieve from the humidity. Even the perpetual haze had disappeared. It was few and far between, this kind of day, so instead of the mile round trip walk, Don added a few more blocks.

Finally, Don and Brownie could see Don's small gray house up ahead. He didn't want the walk to be over with but it was time for dinner.

At the curb Don stopped briefly to survey his well kept yard. It wasn't big by any standard, but it was enough for him. The backyard was slightly larger, good for Brownie, but still small enough for one person to manage.

"I wonder if I should repaint the trim soon." Don said. He eyed the white boarders around the windows and door. Brownie looked up at him.
Sometimes Don pretended that she understood what he was saying. The dog was really his only friend, well, except Jesus. There were nice folks at church, but most of them still focused on temporal things. Not that there was anything wrong with beautiful things and entertainment, but Don was a simple man.

He liked his home clean, uncluttered with trinkets or unnecessary items that just took up space. That was life in general for him. He had a routine and stuck to it. Not for any other reason except that

*The Yellow Note*

he enjoyed privacy and it was hard to find people who shared his devotion to Christ.

"I think I'll wait to paint the trim." Don concluded. He and Brownie started up the short sidewalk and just before they got to the steps he noticed a piece of yellow paper on the doorframe. He took the three steps up towards the house and pulled if off the little rusty nail that it had been punched on to. The paper looked like stationary, unlined and smaller than a standard sheet. It was folded once.

Don opened it.

### *I'LL BE WATCHING YOU*

That was it.

He turned the paper over. Nothing. A small pang of fear hit him, causing him to turn and scan the neighborhood for anything fishy. Directly across the street an elderly couple sat beneath their sun canopy, enjoying the day. He'd met them once in the ten years since living in Raile and couldn't remember their first names. He thought their last name was Fitzger.

A few houses down from them, to the right, was a young mother who sat in a lawn chair reading a book. Her two small children played behind their fenced yard. Elsewhere Don heard the sound of a lawn mower, but everything else was just as it always was.

Don looked down at the paper again.

The letters were bold, written in black marker and formed in block style. Maybe there had been a mistake. Don glanced back at the silver house numbers that hung beside his door. 3848. The eights

*The Yellow Note*

could be taken for threes. But not this close. You couldn't miss it here unless you were blind.

So who did he know who would do something like this? A prankster for sure. He didn't know of any. Someone who was mad at him? Unlikely. Being the homebody that he was there weren't many people who Don conversed with. And anyway, he wasn't one to let his lips flap in every direction. He watched what he said, thought before he spoke. Not shy, just quiet. A listener.

Well, no matter.

He probably wouldn't figure it out right now anyway. No use fretting over something in which he had no details.

Don unlocked his door and let Brownie into the house before him. When he'd locked the door behind him Don crumpled the paper in his hand and was about to bring it to the kitchen waste basket, but then thought better of it. He straightened out the paper and put it in the little drawer in one of the wooden end tables in his living room. Just in case.

Pete found himself zoning out again, this time in his home office to the right of the front entry. He was looking at everything from behind his long oak desk. He'd never really looked around very much before, probably because he was usually too busy. Most of his time spent in this large room was used for study. He had rows and rows of books on crime scene investigation, forensics, criminal profiling and the like. He

*The Yellow Note*

had a more in depth collection than the small library at the police station and proud of it.

Pete breathed investigation. Sometimes while working on a case he would wake up in the middle of the night with an idea and run to his office where he'd spend hours researching and writing notes. Many a case had been solved because of his diligence. That was why he was so well respected at work. Even if the guys didn't agree with his adherence to the Bible, they overlooked it because of his dedication to solving crime.

As his eyes scanned the walls lined with cherry stained bookshelves, he focused in on the farthest wall. It was there his Bible reference sets were, the commentaries and concordances and other books on the Christian faith. A twinge of guilt hit him. He looked away and was saved by a loud noise outside.

Thumping, banging.

Pete got out of his black leather chair and went to the window. He stood close to the clean glass and looked out. Coming up the newly paved horse shoe driveway was a black, two door sports car. A Mustang. The morning sun reflected off the highly polished paint and the chrome rims and details shined like the car was brand new. Even the tires were cleaned and waxed.

The closer the car got, the louder the thumping and Pete realized what it was. Music. If that's what it was called. He rolled his eyes, knowing exactly who it was behind those tinted windows. Chloe Bennett. Heather's best friend. Chloe stopped her car near the front door and waited. She wouldn't get out. She never did before she hauled Heather to school.

And just like clockwork, Heather came bounding down the steps looking pale with bags under her heavily made-up eyes. From where Pete stood he could see the stairs perfectly through the entry. Today, Heather wore black, knee high combat boots with purple nylons and a short black skirt with a black t-shirt and black fishnet on her arms. The fishnet used to be stockings, but she'd cut the feet off and used them as an arm accessory.

Pete never said much about her strange attire, but boy did Kristine lay into her. The woman always gasped in surprise when Heather turned up with some new and bizarre thing. Then she'd launch off into some tirade about how unholy Heather looked.

Of course, Pete agreed, he just kept his thoughts to himself. The less he acted like Kristine, the less Heather seemed to hate him.

He walked to the doorway of his office and stood there, hands in his pockets watching his daughter as she messed with her long auburn hair in a wide golden mirror by the door. She saw him watching her in the mirror.

"What?" Heather continued to pull her hair back into a pony tail then tugged a few pieces out and let them hang in her face.

"Just heard the car pull up." Pete said.

"Hmm." She took one final look and then turned around. "If you're going to say something, just say it." She hoisted her heavy backpack off the floor and put it over one shoulder.

*The Yellow Note*

"Aren't you grounded?" Pete said.

She crossed her arms. "She grounded me from my car. I'm not driving my car am I?"

"Right." Pete nodded. Heather went for the door and Pete followed her.

"You gonna buckle me in or something?" She asked stepping outside the house.

"Just wanted to see what kind of day it was." Really he was going to let Chloe know that he was watching. He couldn't even see the girl behind the dark glass. Heather opened the passenger side door and a blast of sound came out of the vehicle. Screaming, thrashing guitars and thumping bass. Pete cringed.

Heather didn't bother saying goodbye, she just slammed the door and Chloe peeled out. The smell of burning rubber filled Pete's nostrils. He glanced over at the neighbor who was stepping out to get the paper on his sidewalk. The man gave him a disapproving look. Pete forced a smile.

The neighbors probably thought he was a bad father. They probably wondered what kind of show he was running over here. Pete wished Chloe would just not come over. People probably made up all sorts of rumors about him and his family. He sighed and walked back into the house.


The final bell rang Thursday afternoon sending students in a mad race to get out of Don's classroom. He watched as they slapped books closed, shoved

*The Yellow Note*

papers into their folders and sprung up from their desks and ran for the door.

Don stretched in his seat glad to be done as well. He noticed a few of his lazier students copying down the assignment from the board in a hurry. It had been there since the beginning of the hour. Maybe they'd been sleeping. Don focused in on a girl in the back row on the right side of his classroom. Chloe Bennett. She was slumped down in her seat, head draped over the back of the desk like she was sleeping. *How can she sleep like that?*

Her medium length strawberry blonde hair hung in loose waves behind her. It was stringy and un-brushed. Her friend, Heather Monson, was one of the students rushing to copy the assignment down. When she was done, she glanced over at Chloe, saw that she was sleeping and elbowed her friend in the side. Chloe jerked awake and looked around the room in surprise. Don chuckled to himself because of the shocked look on her pale face.

"It's over?" Chloe said. She gathered up her unopened notebook and her small shoulder bag and stood up next to Heather.

"You aren't tired are you?" Heather playfully pushed Chloe and they both giggled as they walked up the aisle together.

As Chloe passed Don she gave him the once over and then locked eyes with him for a few seconds. Strange. Don furrowed his eyebrows as the girls left the room. Chloe was certainly a different human being. There was something about her…he couldn't quite put a finger on it.

*The Yellow Note*

Don glanced around the room and saw a few pieces of trash laying about. He got out of his chair and picked it all up and made sure there weren't any other items left behind by his students. The custodians would be in after a few hours, but Don did the little he could knowing what a long job it could be cleaning a high school.

Don's thoughts wandered far as he circled the classroom and stood in front of the wall of windows. Boy, things certainly were different than he'd expected for himself at the age of thirty-five. Early plans were that he'd be married and have started a family by now. For awhile it looked like things were going to turn out that way.

Those were college days. The days with Aimee. She was a simple girl like him, fun, completely in love with Jesus, just as he'd been. They met during her freshman year, his sophomore year and hit it off right away. She was perfect for him. And one year later he asked her to marry him. She had told him she'd been waiting for the day for a long time and said yes. They made plans to be wed eight months later. That day never came.

Don had started wondering about things a month after the engagement. Aimee seemed to be getting more and more distant from him and then two months after that, just as they were about to mail out the wedding invitations, Aimee bailed. Actually, she turned up pregnant. Don was sure it wasn't his baby, because they'd never been together. Aimee was cheating on him. It wasn't too long after that, Don

33

found out that Aimee and her lover up and left. Don never saw or heard from her again.

He'd been completely lost. He kept asking himself if it was his fault, what he'd done wrong, why it was happening to him. There were no answers. He'd prayed about it, day after day, searching for the reason for all of this. Nothing. His family had tried to comfort him and encourage him, it was hard to pick himself back up.

It was then Don knew he had to leave his perfect little hometown of Jasper and break away from the things he was comfortable with. Since high school he'd been saving for a down payment on a house, he'd had just enough for the little gray house on East Fern Street in Raile, almost 2,000 miles away from where he grew up in Jasper. He didn't have a job yet, friends or even a church, but he felt good about it. It seemed like God was with him. And He was.

It wasn't long at all before Don had found the job as a writing teacher at Beckard High School in Raile, a privet Christian school. And being that Raile's population was nearly 68,000, it didn't take him but three weeks to find good church that he felt completely at home with. Friends didn't come so easily, they never had. Maybe it was because he didn't want to let them in all the way. He was scared of getting hurt again like he had been as a child and by Aimee.

As Don stood at the window in his classroom, he shrugged unconsciously. Even though it wasn't what he'd planned on, it was still good. God was always good to him. He'd always had a roof over his head, food on the table and all of his bills paid. And now

*The Yellow Note*

this teaching position at Raile. He could tell something was different here, way different. It felt just as right as Beckard had, but this go around he felt like he had more purpose.

Even in the few weeks since starting at Raile this school year, he'd already put in hours of prayer for the students and staff he met. There were so many people here who needed Jesus, needed love and help. And of course, there were rules. He couldn't approach a student about religion unless asked and he couldn't be pushy with his faith. Mr. Faulkner, the principal, had really drilled this into Don, especially since he'd come from a Christian school where they had the freedom to speak about religion.

A burst of noise made Don turn from the window. The yelling echoed through the hall outside his room, sounded like girls. He walked across the front of his room and stood in the doorway. He looked right. Nothing. Then left.

At the end of the hall near the stairwell, were two cheerleaders and two other girls. Don knew all four girls, but only by first names. He had a great memory, but there were so many students at the high school, at least ten more per class than what Don was used to at Beckard.

The two cheerleaders, both dressed in their blue and white outfits were Grace and Laura, they stood facing Don. Grace was off to the side by the tan lockers hands over her mouth, eyes wide, starring at the scene. Laura, the other cheerleader, was screaming her head off at the other two girls. Those two girls were Chloe and Heather. The goth girls.

*The Yellow Note*

Don had picked up that lingo just this week having overheard a conversation between Laura and another of her friends during class.

Heather and Chloe were freaks to the high school. Especially Chloe. Don had noticed that everyone seemed to be scared of her, avoided her in the halls and tried not to look her in the eyes. Even the staff. And she wasn't big. In fact, she was extremely thin and short, maybe 5'3".

"You and your friends are all going to hell!" Laura shouted. She kept her head high, using her height as an advantage over Chloe, who seemed to be at the brunt of her irritation. At least for now Heather stood with her arms crossed next to Chloe just listening.

"You're disgusting Chloe." Laura said. "God can't stand you because you're evil." And she spat in Chloe's face. Don could see Chloe's face turn beat red, not from embarrassment, but from rage. She wiped her face and then smeared her hand across Laura's shirt.

"You don't know anything about God." Heather stepped up now. She was about as tall as Laura and even though a bit more timid than Chloe, still very bold.

"And you do?" Laura sneered wagging her head side to side.

Don took a step out into the hall, wondering where any of the other teachers where. Obviously, all the students were out of the building. Oh, that's right. Don knew that the staff all hurried down to the lounge after the bell rang to get the last of the coffee for the day before they went over their assignments for the next day.

He was alone on the second floor. It made him nervous. At Beckard he'd never had to break up a fight, and certainly not between girls.

"You turned away from God you little witch, oops, I'm sorry, Chloe's the witch." Laura put her hands on her hips.

"Shut up Laura, before you make it very, very bad for yourself." Chloe said. She took a step into Laura's space.

"Are you threatening me?" Laura laughed.

"I'm warning you." Chloe said.

It looked like Laura was thinking for a moment, then she said, "Whatever." And she spun around, her long blond ponytail hitting Chloe in the face. She walked towards the other end of the hall where the stairs were and just as she rounded the corner, she yelled,

"Grace!"

Grace looked towards the corner where Laura had disappeared but didn't move. Chloe and Heather left Grace standing there and began to walk towards the other end of the hall. When they passed Don, Chloe looked at him strangely again.

Suddenly, Grace jumped from where she was and ran after the girls, she stopped right in front of them. "What?" Chloe demanded.

"I um, I'm just sorry about Laura." Grace said quietly.

There was a long pause.

"You're kidding." Chloe crossed her arms.

*The Yellow Note*

"No, I'm not. I'm friends with Laura but I don't think she's right treating you like that. I've watched it since school started and I had to say something to you guys."

Don raised his eyebrows. She seemed sincere. Maybe this was the beginning of something good. After all, he'd been praying for these girls. Just like Grace, he'd noticed the constant rivalry that was going on between the two groups of friends.

"Are you getting paid to do this or what?" Chloe asked.

"No," Grace shook her head. "I just wanted to say I'm sorry and I'm not like Laura and her friends."

"Then why to you hang with them?"

"I like cheerleading and they're the first people I met this summer when I moved to Raile." Grace shrugged. Don could tell she just wanted everything to be okay, she didn't want the stupid opposition to continue.

"If you hang with them, you're one of them." Heather said. Both her and Chloe turned away from Grace, walked to the end of the hall and went down the stairs.

Grace stood there for a moment, staring at the floor, looking sad and disappointed. Don was a little disappointed too. Grace finally looked up and saw Don standing there. She gave him a weak smile.

"Hi, Mr. Graham." She said.

"Hello, Grace. I'm sorry your efforts didn't make it further." He told her.

# The Yellow Note

"Yeah." She pursed her lips and looked down at her little watch. "I thought it would be different here at a new school." Her shoulders hung.

"It's just the beginning of the year, things can change."

She nodded. "I have to get to practice. See ya in class tomorrow." She gave him a parting wave and ran off.

Don had guessed right. All the staff from the second floor had hit the teacher's lounge downstairs near the office. It was a large room with sofas and chairs, tables and a TV in one corner on the wall that was currently on a news channel. Two women sat in front of it, half watching, half talking as they sipped coffee. At the back of the room was a full kitchen and a long counter where there were usually doughnuts or cookies and a big urn for coffee. Don was headed there.

He grabbed one of the styrophom cups and turned the spigot on. The coffee came out very dark with grounds that floated to the bottom of his cup. Perfect. Coffee concentrate. He didn't bother to put creamer or sugar in it.

"I wait for the end of the coffee." Said a man in jogging pants and a t-shirt. He wore a whistle on a red shoelace around his neck. He was bulky, not too tall, but good looking. The man had a cup of coffee in his hand too and was leaning against the counter a few feet from Don.

*The Yellow Note*

"Yeah, I like it too." Don said nodding. He took a sip of the coffee. Very bitter. Maybe a little sugar wouldn't hurt.

"I don't think we've met, I'm Al Jurtz," He stuck his hand out. Don shook it.

"Don Graham."

"I teach physical education, health and coach football. I hear you've taken Miranda's place. She was kind of strict. Good teacher though. How are you liking it so far?"

Al looked up at the TV as the sports headlines ran across the bottom of the screen. Don couldn't have cared less about sports. He'd never been much of an athlete. He liked to keep in shape, eat well, but that was it.

"Well, I can't really say yet. It's a whole lot different than the previous school I taught in."

"Yeah? What school was that?"

"Beckard High School."

Al turned back to him, eyebrows raised. "The private school."

"Right." Don wondered if it was considered dorky around here.

"Nice place. My sister went to school there about twenty years ago. They didn't have much of a sports program, so I enrolled in Jethburg. My wife wanted to send our kids to Beckard because of the academic side of things, but we're not very religious. Besides, they're only a few years from high school, I'll be here and I can keep an eye out for them."

*The Yellow Note*

One teacher who'd been reading the paper at a table got up and left the room, mumbling something as she went.

"So, this is where everyone rushes off to when the bell rings." Don said.

Al laughed. "Sure is. I think all of us need a kick in the pants after the day is over. Practice starts at 4:30 this afternoon for me." He looked up at the big clock on the wall. It was 3:30 "We all try to get the last of the goodies before they're all gone. Most of us stick around, try and get some work done here before we have to go home and deal with everything else. I know I can hardly get a thing done with three kids and the wife at home." He shook his head. "You have any kids?"

"No. I'm not married either."

"Just haven't found the right girl huh?"

Don didn't really want to say anything else. Al was just a bit up front for him. "There was a girl...it just didn't work out."

"Life has a way of making things right. I'm sure there's someone else." Al focused in on the TV again.

Don was never much for starting conversation, or even steering them in a particular direction. He'd always admired those evangelists who walked up to anyone on the street to share the gospel with them. Once he'd done it down town and got punched in the face. Since then he'd been afraid to. Not ashamed, he just didn't want to bleed.

*The Yellow Note*

"So," Al began again. "If you ever need any help with anything, I'm on the same side of the hall as you, right when you come up the east stairwell."

Don wasn't sure exactly what he meant. "Help?"

"You know, fights, loony kids..." Al said it was like a usual occurrence. It made Don think of what had just happened in the hallway.

"Oh, right."

"I've never been to Beckard except just in and out, but I'm sure it's not like this school at all. I guess we have the highest rate of violence in the state. And it's not the boys making the record. It's the girls." Al shook his head and finished his coffee, he threw the cup in the garbage next to the counter.

"I just realized that." Don said. Al blinked at him. "Some girls got into it upstairs just a little while ago."

"Let me guess, Laura Thayer and Chloe Bennett." A look of annoyance crossed Al's face.

Don cocked his head. "That would be them. Their friends Heather and Grace were with them. I've never seen girls yell at each other like that before."

"There will be more. Just you wait. Laura and Chloe are both feared around here by the students, just at different ends of the spectrum."

"Why do they hate each other so much?" Don asked.

"Laura's Miss Popularity and she'll do anything to keep it that way, even step on her best friends feet. Chloe doesn't give a rip about anyone except her few friends. Chloe and her friends are the only ones who will stand up to Laura, and it makes Laura furious so

*The Yellow Note*

she does everything she can to make life hell for her. Plus, I guess Laura's all religious or something and Chloe's supposedly into witch stuff. I don't know." Al shrugged. "It's all rumors."

Don was wondering why Laura had said something about Chloe being a witch. Of course, things people say can't always be counted on, but perhaps it was the reason Chloe seemed strange to him. Now that he was aware of it, he'd be able to direct his prayers a little better.

# CHAPTER THREE

Friday at school nothing exciting happened even though Don made sure to keep his eyes open. The weekend wasn't much better. He did his grocery shopping Saturday morning at 8 o'clock a.m. as he did every week, then tended to the front and back lawns, mowing and trimming and weeding. Sunday morning he went to church, enjoying the sermon on the love of God immensely.

Pastor was very passionate about this subject, as well as reaching out to the lost souls of the world. He often taught on both subjects. It made Don feel like going out on the streets too, even though he was scared. One of these times he'd actually do it.

After the Sunday service, Don was invited out to lunch by a group of people who had asked him before. The other times he'd declined, making something up so that he wouldn't have to go. The last time he'd said no, Don later regretted it. Why was he like this? So private and secluded. These were his brothers and sisters, people he would be spending eternity with. He couldn't be like this forever, people

*The Yellow Note*

are everywhere, he couldn't just continue to avoid them for fear of getting too close or getting hurt.

So as hard as it was, Don accepted the invitation to lunch. And he actually had fun. These folks were much more Christ centered than he'd originally thought. And all these years he'd been keeping his distance. What a waste. Don was determined to change that. It wouldn't be easy, but maybe he needed this.

The weekend also brought with it the weather consistent with Raile's southern climate. Thick, humid air and the deep heat. Don woke up feeling the pressure in his head and his strong coffee didn't do the trick. Even Brownie lay on her doggie pillow in the living room looking exhausted.

Don got ready for school slowly because of the heat, and finally had to rush when he realized what time it was. Just before he left, he turned up the wall mounted air conditioner in the living room a notch. He wanted it to be cool when he got home later. And Brownie would like it better too. And finally, he was off in his trusty old Toyota Corolla.

At school he parked in the staff lot, taking his usual space as he did every morning. It was really *his* space too. There was an unspoken rule here that the spot you had on the first day of school was your spot for the rest of year. He'd found out about this rule the hard way. Evidently, the third day of school he'd taken someone's spot. One snippy teacher reminded him that it was *her* spot. Good thing he didn't really care or he'd have given the nasty woman a piece of

*The Yellow Note*

his mind. After that he parked at the back of the lot where he was sure no one had *their* spot.

As he thought about the snippy woman, he wondered if she could possibly be the one who wrote him that yellow note last week. Don pondered it as he walked into the school. That would be silly though. A grown woman writing a note that she'd be watching him? Maybe it wasn't that strange. If girls had fights and yelling matches at Raile, teacher's might be just as weird.

Up in his classroom Don listed his teachings for the day on the chalkboard as students filled the building. As time went on the louder the halls got. Eventually, a few punctual kids came into Don's room and sat down at their desks, ready to learn.

Don was about to sit at his own desk when he heard something outside the window. He left the chalkboard where he'd been and stood at the glass. Yelling. Swearing. Don figured it was another fight and hoped there was someone outside in case things got out of control. He wouldn't make it there in time.

Directly below his window was Laura Thayer, looking upset as a boy from the football team screamed at her. Don couldn't really hear what they were saying through the window. He reached for the crank to open it, paused and finally gave in. He opened the window just enough to listen.

"I can't believe you did this to me!" The boy said.

"James, if you'd just listen to me!" Laura pleaded. She reached for his arm and he pulled away. "I didn't do anything!"

*The Yellow Note*

"I don't want to hear another word out of your lying mouth!"

"Let's talk about lies then." Laura stood up straighter, looking more angry now than sad. "You and Grace. How's that for a lie? You've been messing around with her since summer when she moved here. Don't you think I didn't know about it? And all the time you were lying to my face."

"Don't even compare a mistake I made to what you've done to me. I had to buy a new car, I had to explain to my teachers about all the work I'd been missing…not to mention all the other stuff, all the rumors you spread about me. There's nothing you could say to change the way I feel. We're over." He began to walk away from her and she went after him.

"James, just wait!"

"No. Don't call me, don't talk to me in the hall, don't even look at me." He slapped her hard across the face and she fell over and stayed on the ground in her little cheerleading uniform. She looked humiliated but didn't seem to want to stand up.

"Fine, go have Grace then!" Laura yelled. James didn't even turn to acknowledge that she'd said a word, just kept walking away from his now ex-girlfriend towards the school.

Don closed the window and backed away from it. So maybe this Grace wasn't as innocent as she'd seemed last week when she was trying to apologize to Heather and Chloe. Don chuckled to himself and shook his head. And he was sure he'd find out what Laura had done to make James so mad on the next episode. It was like a soap opera. Why bother

*The Yellow Note*

watching television when you could have a front row seat at Raile High school?

Pete sat in his silver Lexus, engine off, inside his four car garage. He'd had a long boring day at work in a mile high stack of paperwork and having skipped lunch, he was terribly hungry. It was quarter after six and by six-thirty Kristine would have dinner ready. Being the prompt woman that she was, it was always ready on time. If she wasn't home because she was with a client she would leave a note for Steve having prepared everything the night before. If he was at basketball practice or something they all had to fend for themselves. That was happening more often than not these days.

Kristine's car was parked next to his in the second stall. It meant she was probably setting the dishes out on the table. And she was probably still fuming about what happened between them last Wednesday night like she had been the whole week. She was her cute little self in front of others, but to him alone, boy, watch out. Pete moaned to himself. He wanted to eat, but he didn't want to go in there. He really wished there was a case to work right now, then he wouldn't be here, he'd been out on the field or at his desk studying with take-out in front of him. No wife, no kids, just the job. The fun part of the job. He could remove himself from daily life and get lost in the world of investigation.

He had to go in. Kristine would think he'd gone nuts if he stayed out here all night. Pete pushed open

# The Yellow Note

his door and got out. He dragged himself towards the house door and stopped in front of Heather's little red Honda. There was a large dent in the hood. He bent down closer to get a better look at it.

The sporty car had been her sixteenth birthday present to her. The dent hadn't been there then, it was a brand new car. Pete circled the car starting on the drivers side, seeing if there were any other imperfections Heather had acquired. Nothing that he could see. At the passenger side Pete glanced inside the vehicle. It was messy just like her room with clothing in the backseat, pieces of homework laying about and empty pop bottles on the floor.

On the front passenger seat was a stack of books, Pete assumed they were school books but when he saw the title on the top one, he knew they weren't. *Modern Day Witchcraft and Spells.* Chills went up his arms. What on earth did she have that for? Pete pulled on the door handle. It was locked. Why was it locked? If she didn't want anyone inside, then she shouldn't have left the book sitting out in the open.

Now he really didn't want to go inside. He'd have to tell Kristine and she'd flip out and there would be a whole big scene before dinner which would ruin his appetite. He wouldn't say anything. He'd keep it to himself. Yeah. It probably wasn't a big deal anyway. Even though his spirit was urging him to listen to God, he ignored it.

Pete came into the house through the garage door, took his shoes off at the entry like Kristine wanted and heard Steve laughing from his bedroom. He must have a friend over. Pete hung his keys on the little

## The Yellow Note

rack by the door. The smell of beef stroganoff filled the house and he followed the scent to the kitchen where Kristine was hurrying around. She looked at him out of the corner of her eye as she mixed a bowl of salad together.

"Why don't you get Steve and Zack, dinner's about ready." She said curtly. Not even a hi or how was your day. It made Pete stiffen towards her even more. Fine. If she was going to continue in this nonsense, then he would too.

Pete left the kitchen and only got half way up the stairs to the second level when the two boys burst out of Steve's room laughing. When Steve saw that Pete was on the stairs his smile grew even wider.

"Hi dad." He said. "Zack's over for dinner."

"I see that." Pete said.

"Hi Mr. Monson." Zack's freckled face turned down a little. He wouldn't really look at Pete directly. Pete saw why. There was a fresh bruise on his right temple that he was trying to hide with his long brown hair. Instantly Pete thought back to last week when Steve had mentioned Zack might be abused by his mother. Pete regretted not having listened to Steve better then night at dinner. But no one could be sure. Maybe he was just a shy, clumsy kid. Why meddle in other people's business?

"You don't have to call me Mr. Monson, Zack." Pete said.

"Okay." Zack nodded with a grin but still wouldn't look up at Pete.

"What have you boys been up too?"

*The Yellow Note*

"Zack just got this cool video game. Pro Basketball." Steve beamed. He had a hard time finding video games that weren't gory or demonic. It wasn't even Pete's rule, though he completely agreed. Steve just seemed to make good choices without being told.

"Oh, I see."

The boys clomped down the stairs in front of Pete, headed for the dining room. Then Heather came out of her room. She stopped at the top of the steps when she saw Pete there.

"What? You coming to rag on me?" She said.

"No, I was going to get the boys for dinner. I didn't even know you were home."

She cautiously took a few steps down. *Talk to her about the book.* Again, the prompting voice. He didn't want to bring it up and start something. As she passed him he had the sudden urge to hug her. He couldn't remember the last time they'd hugged. But he waited too long. She got to the bottom of the stairs and turned the corner.

Like Pete expected, Kristine acted like everything was just as peachy as pie during dinner. She made a point to talk with Zack, asked him questions about school and how he liked it in Raile. Besides Pete, Heather was the only one who seemed to notice the fakiness in the room. She ate slowly, watching Kristine and even scowled at her a few times while rolling her eyes. Pete almost wanted to encourage it because it was grating on him so badly. It was

*The Yellow Note*

disgusting. He was glad Kristine was sleeping in the downstairs guest room. She could stay there for as long as she wanted. Anyway, why should he apologize? He hadn't done anything. She was the one who treated him like his life didn't amount to anything.

When Heather was finished eating she got up and left without asking to be excused. Pete knew she did this on purpose to bother Kristine. And bother her it did. When Heather got up she left her plate at the table and let the swinging doors go wild as she made her exit. Kristine looked appalled but said nothing. Pete wanted to laugh until he felt a little guilty. Jesus wouldn't think this way. Jesus wouldn't do or think a lot of what Pete had been doing lately.

He shook off the thought and continued eating.

When everyone was finished with the meal, Kristine invited the boys into the kitchen to scavenge for any kind of treat they wanted. She even offered to make them something from scratch. Pete was stunned. Any time he'd asked her to make something fun for dessert she'd complain and moan until he just gave up and stopped asking. She was doing it to get under his skin. He just knew it. So fine, he wouldn't let it bother him. He was full anyway.

Pete retired in the living room at his favorite spot on the sofa, directly in front of the TV. He turned it on and surfed channels, even the religious programming which completely turned him off. They were so...boring. Finally, he found a learning channel that was talking about dinosaurs. It was mildly interesting, enough to keep him there.

*The Yellow Note*

A while later Pete heard the swinging door from the dining room open and the slow foot fall behind him. It was Steve. He leaned against the back of the sofa and watched the television for a second before speaking.

"Did you see it?" He asked.

"See what?"

"The bruise."

"Oh. Yeah, I saw it." Pete turned to his son who looked sad.

"I asked him about it again. This time he said it was because he fell down the stairs at home." Steve came around the sofa and sat down in it.

"Does he ever talk about his family to you?"

"Not really. I know he's got an older sister who pretty much takes care of him. His mom works all the time. I think she's got like three jobs or something. He never invites me over cause he thinks his house is too small. But I just think he doesn't want me to be there when his mom is home and he never knows when that will be cause she works strange hours."

"I feel bad Steve." Pete said. "But I don't know what to do about it. We can't just barge into a person's house and demand to know what's going on."

"Can you find out about his family?" Steve asked

"Steven, you know I can't do things like that. I could be in a lot of trouble at work for taking advantage of our things for personal use."

"I know." He sighed. "I don't know what to do. I pray for him."

"That's really all you can do right now. Keep talking to him, maybe he'll say something and if it

*The Yellow Note*

keeps happening, then we could see about talking to social services. It's possible it's not what you think either Steve."

"What else would it be?"

"I don't know either. You just keep me posted. I'm sure it will all work out."

Zack burst into the room just as Steve got up. With him came the smell of something chocolate. "You should see what your mom did!" Zack said, dragging Steve into the kitchen. Whatever Kristine had done smelled wonderful, but Pete wasn't going to get up. He was going to sit here and pretend like he didn't even know what was going on.

Wednesday during lunch period Don sat behind his desk going over some papers from the morning classes while he ate a roast beef sandwich. He wondered if any of the students paid attention. So far he'd only given out one A and a few B's the majority fell in the C category and the rest were failing or just above it. His red pen would be out of ink soon.

He did have to give them a break though. They were still in the introduction stages of the curriculum and Don was a new teacher too. He wasn't used to the students and they were uncertain about him, testing him out, trying to see if they could trust him. He prayed they would. Don had never just wanted to be a teacher, but a person the kids could look up to, a person they were able to confide in if they had a problem. At Beckard it had been that way.

*The Yellow Note*

Finally, Don gave up trying to correct the papers. He'd finish his lunch and wait until after school to jump back into the heap of papers.

As if on cue, right when Don took his last bite of sandwich, a commotion broke out in the hallway. He listened for a few seconds and heard nothing. Perhaps it wasn't what he thought. These days he was almost expecting a fight. Yesterday there had been one in the school yard between two jocks. It turned out bloody and unresolved.     Of course, it had to be outside the south end of the building, right where all Don's students could see it. In the middle of his lesson, a boy from the row nearest the window stood up and shouted, "Fight!". After that the entire class got up and raced to the window. Don didn't even bother trying to whisk them back to their seats until it was over. Half of them wouldn't have listened anyway, and the other half would have been sitting in their seats, trying to sneak a look.

The noise in the hall started up again.

Don got up from behind his desk and walked to the doorway. It could have been a replay of last week, only this time the scene was a few yards closer to where Don stood and there were several other students walking back and forth. But there they were again, Laura Thayer and Heather Monson. Both of them were shouting at the top of their lungs, spit flying, bodies so close they were almost nose to nose with each other. As far as sheer size, neither girl had the upper hand. It could go either way.

The bystanders were curious enough to watch, but stayed far from the girls as they screamed at each

# The Yellow Note

other. Don couldn't hear anything they were saying because they were all going at it at the same time. Once again, there were no teachers. Except one. Don noticed a woman a few rooms up from him, further from the fight. She peeked out of the little window in her closed door to see what was going on. Don doubted if she could even look that far down the hall from her angle. But she probably had a class going so he'd better do something.

What?

He didn't know how to deal with this. What if they punched him out as he tried to stop it? Sure, he was twice their size, but those red faces and tight fists seemed more than he could handle. That's right! Al Jurtz had offered his bulky manhood to assist Don if he needed it. So Don trotted down to his classroom and found it completely empty. Even the lights were out.

Great. The guy was probably all the way at the gymnasium.

Don said a silent prayer and turned around to face the girls. He began walking towards them, motioning for the other students in the hallway to get out of the way as he neared the girls. His heart pumped, thrashing against his chest, more and more the closer he got.

Don didn't get far before Chloe Bennett came stomping down the tile floors behind him. Her combat boots smacked the floor so hard some of the students jumped and ducked like a gun had gone off.

She passed Don up on the other side of the hall, headed straight for Laura, wound up her arm and socked Laura in the face.

*The Yellow Note*

Every single person gasped in horror including Don. Laura fell into the lockers and slid to the floor, wide eyed. Her cheek was bleeding. She looked to shocked to cry.

Don didn't realize it, but he had stopped.

The whole hallway was frozen and silent too.

Chloe laughed. Don took steps towards them.

Chloe pulled her arm back again and stepped closer to Laura, bending over her like a predator who'd found its prey.

"Chloe!" Don yelled without thinking. He pushed off with one leg and ran for her. Chloe swung. Don clenched his teeth. He had to reach her before she got Laura again. No time! No time!

Right before her knuckles connected with Laura's jaw, Chloe stopped. Her fist was an inch from Laura's chin.

"Just know that it's not over." She growled at Laura.

"Chloe!" Don grabbed her arm and pulled it away from Laura's face. He stood facing Chloe, watching her to see if she would try and overtake him and get to Laura. The look in her eyes scared him. Fierce, evil, destructive. She had the will power to do just about anything, but it didn't look like she was going to attempt another attack. What about Heather?

Don looked over at her, she was breathing hard, staring at Laura, but it didn't appear that she was going to make a move either. Pushing Chloe back, Don reached for Laura and helped her up. Finally, some male staff came running down the hallway, evidently they'd seen the fight on the video monitors

# The Yellow Note

in the office. Both men took Heather and Chloe by the arms and dragged them off to the first floor. The girls protested, demanding Laura be punished as well for her constant antagonism.

Don focused on the injured. "Laura, are you okay?" She seemed off balance and shaky. He noticed that under the fresh break in her skin was the slap mark, probably from James the other day in the school yard.

"I think so." She touched the bloody cheek and began to cry.

"I'll take you to the nurse." Don offered. He led her slowly down the oddly silent hallway, passing students who tried not to gawk but couldn't help it.

"Everything was fine until my boyfriend dumped me." She said. Pictures of Monday's event flashed through Don's mind. "Now all my friends hate me, no one will talk to me. He turned them all against me." She sobbed.

Don wasn't sure what to say to her. He wasn't akin to all this.

"Have you girls had this big of a fight before?"

"A few times…" She trailed off and stopped. "I don't want to go to the nurse anymore. I'm not coming back to school here." Laura sprinted off and disappeared around the corner, leaving Don confused.

What could have possibly gone so wrong for Laura to be so upset that she didn't want to come back to school? Surely, breaking up with a boyfriend wouldn't stop her from coming to school. And this fight with Heather and Chloe, if it happened before, what was the big deal?

*The Yellow Note*

The end-of-lunch bell sounded and a flood of students poured out into the hallway from the few classes that had been in session. A couple of oblivious students bumped into Don so he moved back into his door way and watched the hoard march from class to locker and downstairs. Well, he wouldn't have to wonder what was going to happen during his last class because Heather and Chloe probably wouldn't be there.

# CHAPTER FOUR

Pete huffed all the way down to the high school, gritting his teeth. Everything he did was exaggerated as he slammed his car into park in the visitor lot, got out and clomped in to the office wing of the school.

This was the third time since Heather's senior year started that he'd had to make the trip to school. Twice it had been about her grades and poor attitude, this time he wasn't sure what it was, they wouldn't tell him over the phone. Whatever that insinuated.

In any case, the guys at work were really starting to wonder about Pete's daughter. He probably shouldn't have let on there were any troubles at all with Heather. They probably all thought he was a terrible father.

Pete found his way through the empty halls to the main office. The brunette receptionist looked up at him.

"Can I help you?" She asked.

"Mr. Faulkner called for me, Pete Monson." While the receptionist looked him up in the appointment book, Pete scanned the waiting area. He was glad no one was there. He didn't want to be seen talking to the principal about his kid.

Christians shouldn't have problems like these. His kids were supposed to be good kids, involved in sports, getting good grades, motivated young people.

"Go ahead down to his office. Last door straight ahead." Said the receptionist when she found Pete's name in the appointment book.

Passing a few doors Pete saw Heather sitting restlessly in a small room with a huge plexi-glass window in the side. It reminded him of the interrogation rooms at the office. Heather caught his eye. He looked away.

In the next room Pete saw Chloe Bennett sanding right at the window next to the door, arms crossed, and glaring out at him. He turned away quickly. He'd be a wimp to admit that every time he saw her he felt like running the other direction. There was something about her. Something in her eyes. The devil.

At Bob Faulkner's door, Pete knocked and entered when the man said come in. He looked frazzled. Bob stood up to shake Pete's hand and sat after Pete took one of the chairs in front of his desk.

"Thank you for coming Mr. Monson." Faulkner said in a mildly disturbed tone. He ruffed his balding head of dark hair.

"Sure." Pete looked at his desk and saw a file laying open in front of Bob. Probably Heather's. He wanted to know what was in there.

"I see you're a detective…" Bob patted the file.

*The Yellow Note*

"That's right." Pete nodded, wondering what that had to do with anything. He just wanted to get this over with as soon as possible, get back to work and move on.

"Heather was involved in a fight today during lunch hour in which her friend threatened another student." Bob went on to describe what had happened earlier in the day with great detail.

Pete raised his eyebrows. This was not at all what he'd expected to come and hear. But he wasn't really surprised. It was Chloe. Chloe was always behind the maniac things Heather did. Whether it be sneaking out at night or acting like a complete brat.

"Heather is not in trouble." Bob assured him. "As far as the people who witnessed the incident tell me, she never touched the student who was assaulted."

"Who is the other student?"

"Her name is Laura Thayer. None of the girls are saying how the fight started. All that is beside the point Mr. Monson." Faulkner paused. "I'm not sure if you're aware of it, but Heather's choice of friends seems to have affected her school attendance, her grades and now her public behavior."

Pete sighed. "I'm aware of it." Not that he could do a thing about who Heather chose to hang around with. He and Kristine had tried.

"I spoke with a few of Heather's teacher's today and they all agree she's changed since she started high school here. I called you over to make sure you're up to speed with what's going on. At least on the school end of things."

*The Yellow Note*

Bob looked at Pete like he was wondering what went on at home. "I would hate for such a smart girl to throw her senior year in the drain because of some friends."

"I would hate that too."

"The teacher who witnessed the whole thing, Don Graham, said that Laura has been agitating the girls on purpose, and I have to say that I've seen it myself. Now, while that's no cause for another student to lash out in violence, something must be done at this point."

There was a long pause. Pete was about to get up when Mr. Faulkner pulled a sheet of notebook paper out of Heather's file and slid it in front of Pete. He looked down at the drawings and scribbles that were on the paper and almost choked. Sentences were written in some other language, the pen marks deep and jagged. Scenes of a cheerleader being hung were displayed with a plaque above the noose. *Laura Thayer dies,* it read. There was more where that came from. Knives and guns, bullets whizzing through the air, blood colored in with red pen. So much death and destruction contained on one little piece of notebook paper.

"What is this?" Pete asked.

"This was left under your daughter's desk in one of her morning classes. Today." Mr. Faulkner said.

"How do you know it was hers?" Pete looked down at the page again. It couldn't be Heather's.

"A classmate of hers was going to be snoopy and read it. When the girl saw this, she brought it right down to me. The notebook has Heather's name on

*The Yellow Note*

it, we have the entire thing in a box in another room. We take this sort of thing very seriously here. We are reviewing this with the board and have decided to suspend her from school until further notice. I've already told her."

"Hmm." Pete sighed, he didn't know what else to say. Mr. Faulkner took the notebook paper and inserted it into Heather's file and shut the cover.

"We've also filed a report with the police. Just in case."

Just in case what? Pete was the police! The principal just reminded him of that fact not three minutes ago.

"Is that it then?" Pete asked. He knew he sounded short but right now he didn't really care. A million thoughts were running through his head."That's all." The principal stood. Pete did too. "We have counselors here at the school if Heather needs to talk to someone. She can come in after regular school hours."

"Right." Like she'd talk to them. Pete nodded politely at the man and left the room.

Pete avoided looking Chloe's way as he found meeting room 3 and pushed the door open. Heather got up with her arms crossed and followed him through the school parking lot, no doubt embarrassed that her father was picking her up and dragging her home. Well, it went both ways.

"I'd really like to know what's going on here." Pete asked when they got into his car. Forget trying not to nag. He was angry and at his limit.

"I didn't do anything." Heather mumbled. She refused to look at him.

*The Yellow Note*

"It doesn't matter what you didn't do Heather, it matters that you have a friend who did. Chloe has been a really bad influence on you."

"How the heck do you know it's Chloe, Dad?" She glared at him. If eyes could kill, he'd be dead. "All you do is judge my friends, it's like that's the only thing you know how to do!"

"Judge them? I don't know any of them! The only person you bring home is Chloe and she hardly says a word to us." Pete raced down the neighborhood roads ignoring the 30 mph speed limit signs.

"You and mom hate her, why would she want to talk to you?"

"We don't hate her."

"Then what? You act like she's dirt. So what she doesn't have a bunch of money like we do, or that she isn't Christian, or wear the kind of clothes you think is right. She's my friend. You can't look at outward appearances."

"Heather, it's just…" The words wouldn't form. He wanted to tell her how hard it was being her father. He wanted to unload all the irritation he felt about Kristine and boredom at work and not feeling good enough no matter what he did. But she wouldn't understand and it wasn't her problem anyway.

"It's just what?"

"Nothing, forget it." Maybe he was making too big a deal about it.

Pete merged onto the freeway.

"If it didn't matter you should have just kept your mouth shut." She turned away from him and looked out the window.

*The Yellow Note*

And that was how it was most of the time. Nothing ever got resolved when they talked. As angry as Pete was, he felt sad. His little girl was slipping away. No, she'd already slipped. Was it his fault? No. If it was anyone's fault it was Kristine's for being such a pinch face.

"What was the fight about?" Pete asked.

Heather was silent for a moment and Pete thought it would just be that way till they got home, but she actually answered him.

"It's best left alone."

"Why?"

"Because you'd probably agree with her anyway."

"Try me."

Heather sighed. "She says God hates us, that we're not worth His love, that He doesn't want us. Tells us we're going to hell. Her friends are always making jokes about us, teasing, sometimes pushing...she's the instigator of it all even though every one else thinks we start it. She's such a brat, doesn't deserve to live."

Pete didn't know what it was like to be made fun of. All his life he'd always had many friends and everyone seemed to like him, at least tolerate him.

Wait a minute.

"Did you just say Laura doesn't deserve to live?"

"It's true." She scowled.

"Your principal showed me a piece of notebook paper and—"

Heather cut him off. "He already talked to me about it. He told me I'm suspended." She scowled.

67

*The Yellow Note*

"Why did you draw stuff like that?"

"I felt like it."

"Does it have anything to do with that book I saw laying in the front seat of your car?" There. He'd said it. It really came out without him taking much thought. Maybe that's what it was like for Kristine, she just didn't think before she spoke.

Heather whipped her head around to face him. "You can't just go through my stuff."

"I didn't, it was laying there, I saw it when I walked by." Pete veered into the right lane, making a few other drivers honk at him. He almost missed his exit and had to slam on the brakes to make the turn.

"It's not my book anyway, it's Chloe's. She forgot it there and since mom grounded me from my car, I haven't been inside to get anything. Big deal."

Pete closed his mouth. What was the point of arguing with her about it? She was either lying and wouldn't tell him any part of the truth, or it really was Chloe's book in which case he didn't have to worry about it.

Not worry? But Chloe was Heather's best friend. What she did, Heather did. They were teenagers, every single one on the face of the planet go through stages. This was just Heather's rebellious stage. He'd had one too, of course not quite as drastic as this.

"How long has this fighting been going on?"

"Since I started high school."

"I wish I would have know before."

Pete pulled into their long, driveway and parked in front of the door. Heather gave him a sideways look. A bit surprised, but mostly disgusted.

*The Yellow Note*

"You never ask me how I'm doing, so how would you know?" Her words were like salt in an open wound.

As Heather got out and walked into the house, Pete sat in his car stunned. Boy, was he that out of the loop? He couldn't be that ignorant and inconsiderate. Not to his own child. He shook it off. Heather never spoke to him anymore, that was why he didn't ask her anything, because she never wanted to talk. Why try if it never produced any results? He'd be ready to talk when she was, but not a minute sooner.

# CHAPTER FIVE

Every ten minutes or so Pete looked down at his watch. This time when he saw where the little hands were he groaned and sighed out loud. It was only a quarter to eight. What a drag. He let his arm flop back down at his side, then shoved both hands into his pants pockets.

The pastor's lovely home was full of people, maybe fifty in all at the moment. Since six o'clock people had been flowing in saying hi, having a few snacks and then leaving, some staying longer than others, mainly the families without young children. Pete wished he could leave. Kristine would bite his head off if he did, especially if he left without her.

It was just a regular church social gathering. They happened nearly seven times a year at various large homes of the members that attended The Lord's Fellowship Church. Pete and Kristine had even hosted a few at their house in the previous years. For some reason though, Pete just wasn't into it anymore. The people were the same jolly people, the pastor was the same guy and everyone else seemed in good

*The Yellow Note*

spirits…he didn't know what was wrong with him. Nothing really seemed fun anymore. He'd lost some kind of joy to life. Pete hadn't even been conscious of when it had left, but here he was, standing in the living room of the pastor's house with a bunch of people who were having a good time. He was dreadfully bored.

Pete swirled his glass of lemonade and ginerale mix around and stared at the pieces of pulp that floated around in circles. He kept swirling. Round and round. Might taste good with a shot of liquor. Suddenly, Pete stopped the swirling motion. What was he thinking?! He'd not had a taste of alcohol since his freshman year of college just before he'd gotten born again.

After drinking the rest of what was left in the glass, Pete meandered through the sea of bodies to the kitchen where he found the counter and set the glass next to all the other dirty ones. He noticed Kristine outside the kitchen window. She was standing on the other side of the large deck with a few of her girlfriends from church talking. All four girls were laughing, making exaggerated hand motions and expressions. Pete used to laugh like that with her. Pete hadn't laughed with anyone much lately.

Feeling even lower than he had a few minutes ago, Pete left the kitchen and wandered to a more quiet part of the house. The Pastor's study. He stood in the doorway for a second, looking in. There weren't any lights on in the room, but the light from the entryway was enough to see.

*The Yellow Note*

It was a long room, high ceilings and crowned molding, high bookcases and hardwood flooring. An antique runner stretched across the floor with a comfortable looking sofa and chairs on top of it.

"This is my favorite room in the whole house." Pastor's voice came from behind Pete. Pete turned and smiled at the sixty-three year old man.

"It's nice." Pete said. "I've always admired this room."

"That's forty-eight years of book collecting there." The Pastor walked into his study gazing up at all the shelves of books. "I love reading and studying. Especially, God's word."

"Hmm." Pete nodded and took a few steps into the room. The pastor sat on the edge of his big, mahogany desk.

"You feeling alright?" The pastor asked.

Pete had to think about that one. Physically, just fine, peachy. Mentally...exhausted. Did he want to start up this conversation here when all these people were looming around the house? Did it really matter?

"I don't know." That was the best he could do without much thought.

"Kristine confided in Jeannie the trouble you two have been having with Heather."

Pete hung his head down and plopped himself into one of the chairs in front of the desk. "She's uncontrollable. It's put a distance between me and Kris...I don't know, maybe it's not just Heather, but she doesn't make anything any easier around the house."

*The Yellow Note*

"Have you two talked about this? I mean *really* talked."

Pete paused for a moment. No. Not *really.* But what was there to talk about? "Heather doesn't listen to either of us, there isn't much we can do about it. I wish she were more like Steve, he's such a good kid, I never have to scold him for anything, he makes good decisions, obeys our rules."

"Are you carrying through with punishment if Heather fails to abide by the rules you lay down?" Pastor stared hard into Pete's eyes. Almost felt like he was peeking around in his soul. Pete looked away. He couldn't lie. What would be the point anyway?

"It's hard. She freaks out if we discipline her harshly. And she seems good at finding ways around being grounded or around certain privileges we take away. Most of the time she pretends that she doesn't care if she's grounded." Pete shrugged.

"You know, you can't compare Heather to Steve, they are totally different kid's." Pastor said.

"I know." Pete nodded. "I'm just not sure how they turned out so different."

"Even the smallest circumstances change the outcome of a person's life. I remember you told me she doesn't have the greatest friends. The Word says that good company corrupts bad character. If Heather is spending all her time with a poor choice of friends, she isn't going to be following a good example." Pastor said.

"It doesn't matter if we tell her she can't hang out with certain people. She goes ahead and does it anyway."

*The Yellow Note*

The pastor pursed his lips and sighed. Pete didn't know if that was a good thing or a bad thing, but he waited until the man spoke again.

"How much time do you spend at work?"

Pete frowned. Great, now he was sounding like Kristine. "I don't know, the usual."

"And what is that?"

"Between 45 and 50 hours a week. More if there's a big case. Kristine works about the same."

"How much time do you spend with Heather and Steve?"

Pete groaned inside and clenched his jaw. This wasn't how he wanted the conversation to go.

Just as he was about to defend himself, his cell phone buzzed at his hip. He pulled it up and looked at caller ID. It was his boss, Frank. Pete flipped open the phone and put it to his ear.

"I have to take this." Pete said to the pastor. "Hey Brad." Brad Cohan was another homicide detective that Pete worked with.

"Pete, where are you?" Brad asked. He sounded like he was walking or something.

"I'm at a party." Pete stood up and eyed the pastor who was waiting patiently.

"There was a murder at the Whitmore Estates. 15785 Gilbert Lane. Crime lab is down there already, Frank wants us in lead. I'm driving there now."

"Okay, I'll be there." Pete shut his phone and put it back into his pocket. The pastor looked at him a little disappointed but still smiling.

"Maybe we should have coffee sometime." Pastor said, standing up from the edge of his desk. The man

*The Yellow Note*

was so kind, it was hard for Pete to leave. And he had so much stuff on his shoulders...

"Yeah, maybe that would be good." Pete nodded and shook the pastor's hand before he left the room.

Pete rushed through the house and was almost to the front door when he realized he hadn't told Kristine that he was leaving.

With a heavy sigh and rolling of the eyes, Pete turned around and walked towards the back of the home. On the way a few people tried to talk to him but he just smiled and kept going. He'd probably hear about it later from Kristine after the same people asked her if something was wrong with him. Those busybodies could keep their gossip going. Even if you were perfect they'd find something to rag on. Jesus probably even fell under scrutiny in their little group.

Kristine was talking with the same women that she had been with earlier, but this time they were talking more seriously. He exited the back door slowly and stepped onto the deck where they were, feeling unwanted and out of place. When she heard the squeak of the screen door, Kristine turned.

"Hi Peter." She said. Sometimes she called him his full name when she was irritated, but her friends didn't know it. They all just looked over at him making him feel even more uncomfortable. They had probably just been talking about him.

"I have to go to work." Pete said quietly when he got closer to her. Kristine looked at her watch and her smile quickly faded. She motioned for him to follow her to an empty side of the deck. He did, reluctantly, because he knew what was coming.

*The Yellow Note*

"As upstanding members of the church we should be here till the party is over Peter." Kristine glared at him, facing away from the other ladies so they didn't get a glimpse of her bad temper. Pete wished they'd see it one of these days, then they'd know that Kris was more than just a kind, loving woman.

"There was a murder Kris. I have to do my job, I don't have a choice." He said it quietly. "Do you want me to quit and stay home all day, make no extra money for us?"

Kristine grit her teen and narrowed her eyes. She knew he didn't have a choice. From the second Pete became a detective she'd know it.

"Fine then, go." She turned from him and instantly changed her face for her three girlfriends who didn't seem to think anything was wrong at all. They all carried on like Pete had never come out to talk with Kristine.

Pete stared at the back of Kristine's head. Who was that woman? Did he even know her?

Pete pulled up behind Brad Cohan's dark gray Bronco and parked. The entire block was filled with emergency vehicles and barricaded off with officers standing at each end checking who came through. They all knew Pete and all he had to do was nod.

Up and down the street onlookers watched as they stood on their front lawns, some with disturbed looks on their faces, others hoping to catch a glimpse of the body or glean some more information. The media was not allowed on to the street with their vehicles

*The Yellow Note*

or their crew. From behind the road blocks they reported, cameras zooming in as far as they could, getting at least the action surrounding the house.

Pete stepped out of his car and was immediately greeted by the police commissioner Frank Adison. The man was of short stature, but had a big, barrel chest and was thick all around. He had dark hair, dark eyes and a sinister looking goatee. At the very least he was intimidating. Even though most of the men at the police station were taller and more muscular than Frank, his presence demanded a sort of fearful respect.

He was a good man though, and fair. Every single man on the force trusted him with their lives.

"Pete, you got here mighty quick." Frank said as he hiked his slacks up over his bulging stomach. He'd loosened his collar and tie already, something he only did when things were crazy.

"Yeah, I was at a church party near by." Pete glanced up at the house. The lawn was busy with people from the forensics team. They were probing the grass, taking pictures of what may end up providing key pieces to catching a suspect.

"Did Brad brief you on the phone?" Frank asked.

"No."

"Okay, I'll do it. Then I gotta run." Frank cleared his throat. "Seventeen year old girl, Laura Thayer." Frank continued to speak but Pete zoned out, remembering the girl's name. Wasn't she the one Chloe and Heather had a spat with just a few weeks ago? Pete tried to listen to Frank, it probably seemed like he was, but he was also trying to retrieve details form his mind about Laura.

An image of Heather's notebook with Laura's dead body in it suddenly came into Pete's head. It almost made him flinch.

"Pete." Frank was starring at him.

"Yeah." Pete snapped back to reality, a million thoughts still flashing through his head.

"Where'd you go?"

"Oh, nothing. Sorry, I heard you." He lied. He could just get the info later from Brad.

"I think Brad's in the driveway." Frank said scanning the faces and finally looking in on the blond haired man talking to an officer. Even in the dark Brad looked like a beach boy. He just didn't fit the investigator mold. He should be on a tropical beach somewhere, surfing or sipping a coconut drink in the sun. It was probably why all the women at the station swooned…until they found out what kind of man he really was. A player.

"Okay."

"See ya." Frank hurried off down the street to find his vehicle.

Pete walked up the driveway to where Brad was. The other officer made one quick statement to Brad, nodded politely at Pete before he answered his squawking radio and bolted down the drive and got into one of the squad cars in the street.

"Hey Pete." Brad smiled wide, his recently whitened teeth gleaming in the pulsing blue and red lights from the police vehicles. He gave Pete a friendly

*The Yellow Note*

punch to the shoulder. The guy couldn't help himself. He was a complete jokester and buddy to all.

"What's going on?" Pete asked.

Brad chuckled. "I saw you staring off when Frank was talking to you."

"Are you going to tell me or what?" Pete grinned a little. Even though Brad was very worldly and didn't believe in Jesus, he sure was lively. It rubbed off on the other guys, Pete too.

"Laura Thayer. Seventeen. Attends Raile High school." Brad paused a second. "Hey, doesn't Heather go there?"

"Yep." Pete didn't want to tell him that he'd been thinking about Heather in relationship to Laura. The guys at work knew he left early Wednesday to get Heather at school, but he'd been embarrassed to tell them why. Now he was glad he hadn't said anything.

"Anyway, we can probably go in soon. The crime lab is almost done—"

"Almost done?" Pete interrupted, shocked at the quickness of the procedure.

"Uh-huh. I'm telling you buddy, this place is as clean as a whistle. No physical evidence to speak of. At least not since I talked with one of the guys about an hour ago."

"How long have you been here?" Pete looked at his watch. It was almost 9:30.

"A few hours." Brad grinned and crossed his arms, tilting his head back slightly like he'd just mounted a high horse.

*The Yellow Note*

"Really?" Pete was stunned. Brad had a propensity to be late for everything.

"I was at the office when the call came in. I told you we're leading the team right?"

"Yes. What's so clean about this place?" Pete looked up at the large home. It was a beautiful white structure with giant columns and vines growing up the siding, trimmed only over the windows.

"No foot prints, no sign of forced entry. Nothing glaringly obvious. The Thayer's have a very thorough housekeeper who is currently being questioned at the station. The windows are spotless, door handles wiped clean, even smells clean in there. I guess today was her day to tidy up." Brad said.

"Who called emergency?" Pete asked.

"Laura. She didn't actually speak to anyone, they traced the call."

Just then one of the guys in a jacket labeled 'Forensics' waved at Brad from the front step. "All clear Brad, we're finished for now."

"Okay, thanks." Brad looked at Pete. "Let's go." They followed the driveway up to the sidewalk and up the steps.

They both went inside making their way to the living area. Pete stood at the edge of the carpet on the oak wood flooring looking over the whole scene. The place was covered in blood, lamps and furniture out of place and broken. It was the goriest thing he'd seen in a long time. It made him want to turn away and pray.

The teenage girl lay on the off white carpet in her own blood, legs in an awkward position. There was

*The Yellow Note*

no doubt at least one of them was broken. In her hand was the portable phone, still grasped tightly.

Pete felt his chest tighten, his heart beat rapidly. Heather's crude drawing came to his mind again. Of course, Laura wasn't hung by the neck in this house, but here she was, dead. It made Pete feel a little sick to his stomach.

"We're gonna have the Thayer's security system company check to see if the thing was working properly, but as far as we can tell, it's a-okay." Brad said, He walked in further towards the body.

"So whoever was here had to know the code." Pete said.

"Right."

"This looks like more than one person." Pete said scanning the scene.

"Or one person who went completely nuts." Brad answered.

Pete nodded. Things were a disaster in the house. Almost everything was broken, ripped or damaged in some way. Even the walls had holes in them."

"Hey, I just remembered." Brad paused and put his hand to his face. Forensics collected a piece of paper that was pinned to the big oak tree out front. Said something like, *I always knew you were a hypocrite. What a shame Laura.*"

"On the front tree?"

Brad nodded. "A small piece of lined, yellow paper with black, block style lettering." Brad paused and looked around.

"Where are her parents?" Pete asked.

*The Yellow Note*

"The mother flipped out, she was admitted to the psychiatric ward. Her husband is with her. We'll talk to him there."

# CHAPTER SIX

"I don't know what to tell my other two daughters." Richard Thayer said. His face was ghostly white, eyes bloodshot and tired. "Neither of them have any idea. In fact, they are planning to drive to Raile tomorrow night for her surprise birthday party that we've been planning."

Pete waited for him. Over the years he'd gotten used to letting his interviewees talk until they ran out of words. Sometimes it was boring, but more often than not Pete was able to pull some useful information from their otherwise useless babble.

Richard, Pete and Brad sat in a small waiting room in the psychiatric ward of St. Francis Medical Center. It wasn't half bad like some of the other psychiatric hospitals Pete had encountered. Here it was newly re-carpeted, re-painted and all the furniture and decorative items well kept. The staff was pretty friendly too. But Pete was sure Richard wouldn't have allowed his wife Susan to be hauled off to some creepy place.

*The Yellow Note*

"We were going to have the party at Laverie's, close down business for one night just to do it." Richard closed his eyes and shook his head.

Richard owned a chain of high class restaurants called Laverie's after his Italian father's first name. The restaurant served fine Italian food, mostly recipes of his father's. "I just don't know what to do." Richard said. "I'm sorry."

"It's okay." Pete said.

"Okay, I'm ready. I'll answer any questions you guys have if I can." Richard nodded and took a deep breath and straightened his large frame in the small chair he sat in.

"The first thing we'd like to try and figure out is whether or not she had any enemies." Brad said. He was holding his trusty little notebook, it's pages terribly wrinkled and dirtied. He took more notes than anyone Pete knew. Pete himself had a small but hardly touched pad of paper. He had a good memory, but just in case always had a pen ready.

Richard took a minute to think. "She had a way of making many enemies."

"How so?" Brad asked.

"Well, I think she was spoiled." Richard shook his head and sighed. "My fault. I was poor as a kid and had to work really hard to get what I have now. I wanted to give my kids everything, I held nothing back. My two eldest girls seem to be pretty level headed, but Laura was a bit more greedy."

He pursed his lips. "I can't believe I'm saying this all in past tense." He sighed once more and continued. "Laura chose to flaunt herself, her things, bragged about it. She made a lot of her classmates mad because of it. I can't count how many times she's had a friend over and they got into an argument over something menial. But Laura was a manipulator and she got what she wanted, even from people she made angry. Eventually they all became her puppets. And if they wouldn't bow down to her, they became her enemies."

"Anyone who may have gotten so fed up with her that they would go to drastic means to stop it?" Pete asked.

"One girl at school never took crap from Laura and they both clashed constantly. The girl attacked Laura a few times, once just recently."

"Do you remember the girl's name?"

"I think her name is Chloe. I'm not good with names. I should remember too cause we pressed charges once, but after that things just got worse for Laura. I guess this Chloe or whatever her name is, and her friend sort of upped their forces against Laura."

Pete just stared at Richard, his lip turning up. He didn't have to write Chloe's name down. Every time he heard Chloe's name, he cringed. Bad things just followed her no matter where she went. Instantly, Pete found himself honing in on her as a very clear suspect. Whether it was right or not, he was ticked. Ticked that his own daughter could be hanging around a murderer.

"How long has this been going on?" Brad asked.

"Years, at least since junior high. For awhile everything was okay. I mean before all of this. She had a friend who was religious and Laura went to

*The Yellow Note*

camp with her one summer and came back saved... or whatever you call it." Richard grunted.

"Anyway, for the rest of that summer Laura was like a different person, nice, thoughtful...then her friend moved away and they lost contact. Slowly, Laura began to act like the old Laura, actually worse. I don't know why I'm saying all of this, it's probably not relevant at all."

"No, no." Pete shook his head. "We never know what ends up being relevant. It's quite alright. Anyone outside of school that we should look at?"

"You mean enemies? Not that I know of." Richard leaned forward on his knees and stared down at the dark blue carpet beneath him. "It may be nothing, but like you said, some things mean more later..."

He looked up at Brad, then at Pete. "Laura broke up with her boyfriend James not too long ago. She wouldn't tell us much about it, said she was embarrassed. I've never known James to be a violent person, but that day Laura had a huge red mark on her face."

"James hit her?" Pete asked.

"She didn't say. Just ran past me quickly up to her room. I asked if everything was okay and all she said was that her and James had broken up."

"He goes to Raile high school?"

"Yes."

Pete nodded. He jotted down a few notes about a possible interview with this James.

"We also found a yellow note tacked to a tree in your front yard." Brad said. He was shaking his left foot, eyes intensely focused in on Richard. Pete had

88

*The Yellow Note*

tried to coach him a bit on how to keep his cool during an interview, but the guy simply couldn't remember. He had so much nervous tension built up inside, the drive of the job just eating at him to get moving that he had to let it out somewhere. His foot.

Richard cocked his head and blinked. "What note?"

"On the big palm near the end of your drive. Five by eight yellow stationary. It said, I always knew you were a hypocrite. What a shame Laura. "

Richard's face turned down even more, but then his eyes changed. "There was a note, yellow, strange letters, square or boxy like. I found it on the kitchen table. Laura had brought it home. She'd found it in her locker. When I asked her about it she had no clue who'd put it there."

"What did it say?"

"I'll be watching."

Pete raised his eyebrows and looked at Brad

"Were there any others?" Brad asked.

"Laura said one had showed up under the windshield wiper of her car. She didn't tell us what was on that one. Just made some comment about the jerk who wrote it, that they'd better mind their own business. As far as I know those were the only two, but towards the end here Laura had become kind of quiet, wouldn't tell us much." Richard looked sad about that.

"How long ago was that?" Brad said.

"The first one about a month ago, the second a week later." He looked from Pete to Brad and back again.

*The Yellow Note*

"Would it be alright Richard if we took Laura's cell phone to check her messages and calls and text messages?" Pete asked.

"Sure." He nodded. "I don't know where it is, maybe her room or her purse."

Pete reached into his shirt pocket and pulled out a card and handed it to Richard. "We'll let you get back to your wife now. When you think she's coherent enough, give us a call. And if you think of anything, even if it may seem insignificant, call."

All three men stood up.

"Okay." Richard nodded, holding the little card like it was something very valuable. They all shook hands before Pete and Brad left.

Early mornings were always peaceful at the high school. The halls were silent except for the occasional footfall of other staff members on the freshly waxed floors. Today was an exceptionally quiet morning, but not peaceful. All the teachers had been called in early for a staff meeting about Laura Thayer. They had all been instructed to send any students in need of counseling to the office where the principal had set up a team of staff ready to help.

As soon as the meeting was over, Don made way to his classroom where he spent some time in prayer for Laura's family and friends. Eventually, it was time to busy himself with the daily routine.

Don went through his desk searching for any trash or things that were out of place, something he did every morning. Being that he almost always put

*The Yellow Note*

things away the minute he finished using them, it was a rare thing to find a misplaced item, and even more uncommon for him to spot a piece of garbage.

When that was over Don went to arranging his lesson for the day. It was short and needed minimal preparation. By 7:40 Don had everything ready. He rocked in his chair for a moment, eyes wandering around the room. His gaze finally rested on Chloe's desk. It was marked up in every way, deep gouges in the top, pencil lines, permanent marker drawings and some other indentations Don swore were teeth impressions.

He shook his head unconsciously with a slight smile. Chloe amused him. Over the ten years of high school teaching there was always one student that filled this role. But none quite as fitting as Chloe. There was something new everyday with her. From falling asleep in class to her strange attire to having an all out fit in front of her peers. It certainly kept his last hour class interesting.

Suddenly, Don felt a pang of sadness for her. She was obviously crying out for something. Her recent overdose came to mind. Just a few weeks ago she'd passed out in the hallway just feet from his room, completely unconscious, but tears streaming out of her eyes. Having been the only one around at the time Don had prayed for her before other teachers came to his aid and whisked her away before he'd had a chance to do anything more. What an awful thing to have witnessed. Worse than all the fights he'd encountered recently.

It was that day he'd made a point to look over her school records, see if he could understand her better.

*The Yellow Note*

Indeed the file was thick and rich with negative incidences. Chloe had been a good student without bad report until the age of thirteen when it all changed. She'd become belligerent in class, her grades fell and there were multiple accounts of her violent behavior. After having a talk with the principal, Bob Faulkner, Don found out that Chloe's parents had both died in a place crash when she was thirteen.

No wonder.

If the other students knew this, surely they wouldn't treat her so poorly, but they had to know about it. Chloe had grown up here.

"She's dead?!" A female voice broke Don's train of thoughts. The words came from the hallway. He turned to look, but couldn't see anything from where he sat behind his desk. Then there were sobs and the sound of books hitting the floor.

Don stood up and walked to his door where he saw two students to the left. One of them was Grace Hartson and the other, star sports guy James Riley, Laura's ex-boyfriend.

"When?" Grace asked. Her body was shaking, face red, mascara running in streaks down her pale skin.

"Last night." James said. He put a hand on Grace's shoulder. Don noticed the school books laying face down, open and a notebook and some pens scattered about on the floor. Grace's little black purse was to her right, tipped over, the contents spilling out. Evidently, the news had so shocked her she dropped everything.

"Oh my gosh." She gasped. "What happened?" Her lips quivered. A few other students passed by her,

*The Yellow Note*

staring, but seemingly unaware of what she'd just discovered. Most of the students probably wouldn't know about the murder until first class began. All the teachers had also been instructed to announce the new in a respectful manor to their students. Don wasn't looking forward to it.

"I guess she was murdered." James said quietly.

"Murdered!" Grace squealed. Her knees gave out and she fell to the floor where her things lay. She put her hands on her head and ran her fingers through her short, spiky brown hair. "I can't believe it." Grace balled, her hands now running down over her face, smearing the make-up even more. James knelt down beside her, his face anguished as he tried to comfort her.

"I can take you home." He said. She nodded, but continued crying. James started to help her up when two girls in cheerleading uniform came running up behind them.

"Did you hear about Laura?" The one said, her face also red from crying. James simply nodded, pulling Grace up and holding her tight.

"I'm taking Grace home." He told them, obviously hinting that they move out of the way.

"We're canceling practice today Grace." The other girl said. Both of them hugged Grace, then let her leave with James.

The girls stood in the hallway looking dazed. "It's unreal." The one said.

"I know."

"I heard that the police think someone from school did it."

*The Yellow Note*

"Really? How do you know?"

"I don't know." She shrugged. "It's just what I heard."

"I wouldn't be surprised if it was Chloe Bennett. Those two have been at it since forever."

"Yeah." The one girl paused looking down at Grace's stuff. She bent down and started picking it up. "Not to be weird, but maybe now things will calm down a bit with Laura out of the picture."

The other cheerleader baulked at her friend. "I can't believe you just said that, Laura was our friend."

"I'm just saying, Laura was bratty. She's the one that started things with Chloe most of the time. Maybe it'll get those freaks to stick to their own deal."

"I still can't believe you're thinking about that right now. Our friend is dead."

There was a long silence.

"I wasn't really her friend." She clutched Grace's books close to her chest. Then she looked up at her friend. "Don't tell me you really liked her...I mean you were just saying how you didn't want to be involved with Grace's plan for Laura's surprise party?"

"Yeah, but..."

"I don't even know why Grace liked Laura so much. All Laura did was talk behind her back."

"Laura talked behind everyone's back though. Grace is new, she just didn't know what Laura was really like."

"I'm sad and all cause you know, she's dead, but seriously, I bet it'll be a lot less uptight now."

*The Yellow Note*

"This is so weird."

"Hmm."

"Now what?"

"I don't know, I feel sort of ill."

Both girls walked off, carrying the dramatic scene with them. Don noticed that the other students in the hallway seemed to have no idea that something bad had happened.

Don stepped backwards into his classroom, tears welling up in his eyes. He wished he were home so he could get on his face and pray. His whole body was filled with sorrow. Oh how he hoped that Laura had known the Father. How were her parents doing? How could anyone find the words to console them?

Suddenly, Don hurried across the hall to the restroom. Thankfully, it was empty and he closed himself in a stall and broke down to pray, the words spilling out as rapidly as his tears.

The staff lounge was packed with teachers and office aids. Someone spoke quietly, but everyone was reverent as they all watched the television in the corner of the room. The local news channel was on, covering the investigation of Laura Thayer's murder.

Don stood in back near the snack counter, coffee in hand not having even taken a sip yet. It was getting cold, but he didn't notice. Al Jurtz was silent next to him. Don made a heavy sigh and focused on the news again half listening, half thinking. As the anchor woman spoke, something caught his attention.

*The Yellow Note*

"...a piece of yellow stationary found on one of the palm trees in the Thayer's yard. Though authorities are not yet revealing that exact content of the note, it is believed to be a death threat targeting Laura." The woman moved on to another subject involving the murder, nothing Don was interested in at this moment.

Yellow stationary?

Don glanced at Al who was frowning at the television shaking his head slightly. "Al." Don said.

"Yeah." The man kept his eyes forward.

"Did you hear the whole bit about that yellow paper they found?" Don felt kind of stupid asking, he should have been paying attention.

Al turned to him. "Just what they said right now."

"Right. I zoned out for a minute. What exactly were they saying."

"I guess Laura had gotten one in her locker just last week too."

Al looked back at the TV..

Don forced himself to be calm. There was no reason to get worked up just because he'd received a note as well. He shouldn't worry about it anyway, the Bible was clear about worry. Don't do it.

Finally, Don dumped the rest of his cold coffee down the sink behind him and threw the Styrofoam cup in the garbage. He left the room and it's sadness. It was time to go home and pray.

There was yellow by the door again.

*The Yellow Note*

Don sat in his car, staring up at his house eyes fixed on the piece of yellow paper on the door frame. He really didn't want to get out. He wanted to lock himself in his car and drive away. But Brownie was in there, she would need to be let out after being cooped up all day long. What if *they* were inside.

No.

Don took a deep breath and pressed his eyelids together. "Lord, you tell us not to worry, it's really hard right now, but please, help me not to."

Reaching into his back pocket, Don pulled out his cell phone. He'd call the cops right now, have them come, scope the place out and make sure everything was okay. He flipped open the phone and started to press the number for information when a strong sense came over him.

*STOP!*

The word was so clear he actually jerked, the phone almost sliding through his fingers to his lap.

*Just let it be.*

If at anytime he'd heard the Spirit of God speaking loud and clear it was now. "Just let it be?" Don said. "Are you kidding me?" He looked at his phone, the number he'd pressed in waiting to be sent. "If I don't call the police...what if something happens...I could be murdered!"

*Don't you trust Me?*

Don closed his mouth.

His heart fell silent and he nodded as he stuck the phone back into his pocket. He really didn't want to do it this way. It was hard for him to even move knowing that he'd have to go up to that door, take the note off and read it again. And why? Why on earth was Jesus telling him to forget calling the cops? It seemed absurd!

But obviously God knew more than he did. He had to trust Him. He had to be obedient. If not now, when would he ever listen to the Holy Spirit and do what He asked?

Acting as if everything was normal, Don grabbed all his things from the car, locked it and marched up the sidewalk to the door. He unlocked that, ripped the note from where it was on the door frame and went inside. After locking the door behind him Don stood in the entry, glancing around his living room.

Where was Brownie?

Her doggie bed near the window was empty, a smashed down area on it where her body once lay. Then he heard clicking. Brownie appeared in the hallway, tongue hanging out of her mouth.

Don let himself relax.

If Brownie was okay and she wasn't freaking out, no one was in the house. He was fine.

Don set his things down on a chair and then held up the note. Same as before. Same paper, same writing.

### *SO FAR SO GOOD*
### *DON'T LET ME DOWN*

"What?" He said out loud, reading the note a second time. It just didn't make sense. Don't let me down? Another round of panic waved over Don. Don't let who down? What was he doing that could

*The Yellow Note*

be so disappointing? And if he let whomever down, what would they do? Had Laura let someone down? Is that why she was dead.

Brownie whined and took a few steps closer to Don.

He pet her head. She could probably sense his accumulating worry.

"Okay, Lord, I have no idea what You're trying to do here, but I have to be honest, I'm scared and I need Your Spirit to help me not be. If you still want me to forget about the cops, then I will, but I don't like it."

Don waited. Nothing.

Well what did he expect, he already knew what God had said. Don pulled open the little drawer in the end table next to the sofa and set the second note on top of the first one. Just in case.

"Forensics pulled a blue, glass water bottle out of the house." Brad said when he looked away from his computer screen. He always sat so close to the thing, no wonder he complained about eye strain.

Pete shuffled through some papers at his desk which was butted up against Brad's at the front. Frank always teased them about it, but it was a good way to work not having to break his neck every five minutes when they had to share information.

"A water bottle?" Pete continued searching for the notepad he'd somehow buried beneath everything.

"Yup." Brad paused to watch Pete. "Did you lose something?"

*The Yellow Note*

"Remember that woman, Helen something or other, the guys downstairs took a message cause she wouldn't talk to anyone but us..." Pete frowned. Frustration was building. Life just wasn't going right for him, not with Kristine or Heather and now he was loosing things.

"Didn't you write it down?"

Pete didn't answer him. If he had, it would have come out agitated.

"You never lose stuff." Brad smirked and put his feet up on his desk. "Maybe my ways are rubbing off on you."

Pete moaned. "That number was really important. I have to find it. That Helen woman is the only lead we've got right now."

"Don't spazz out buddy. It'll turn up." Brad cocked his head at Pete. "You're really bent out of shape, what's going on?"

"Nothing." Pete mumbled. Now he was just going over the same things on his desk, trying to avoid eye contact with Brad.

"It's Kristine isn't it." Brad chuckled. "Women will do that to you, that's why I just can't get serious. Plus, it's too much fun trying to pick up girls at the bar. Even if I don't go home with them, the challenge is great."

*That's disgusting.* Pete looked at Brad. *How can the guy feel good about himself?*

"Kristine is fine." He lied. "Everything is fine, I just want to find that number."

"The blue bottle may mean more than whoever this Helen chick is." Brad said. "The lab found prints on the glass."

*The Yellow Note*

Pete stopped his searching. "Clean?"

"Perfect." Brad nodded, a glimmer in his eye. "I never saw the bottle when we were in there, I guess when forensics combed through the living room they found it under a table. There's half moon impression in Laura's forehead. I saw it myself this morning when I went to check out how far Mick had gotten with the examination. Looks like a bottle imprint to me."

"Did you see the bottle?" Pete asked. He plopped down in his chair. Suddenly the note he was looking for took a back burner.

"Uh-huh. I didn't measure or anything since the lab will, but it looked roughly the same size as the impression on Laura's skin. The bottle had a little blood on it too." Brad said.

"The murder weapon. One of them at least. Did you ask if they had a chance to print the other things in the room?"

"They did. Where were you this morning anyway, you got here later than me?" Brad asked.

Pete wasn't about to explain the yelling match that Kristine and Heather had last night at about 1:30. "Didn't sleep well last night." He said. It seemed like enough for Brad. Good.

"Were they able to find a match with those prints on the bottle?" Pete asked.

"No match." Brad shook his head. "Went through the system without a single hit."

"Hmm."

"I found Laura's cell phone too." Brad smiled and picked up the little purple phone and handed it to

Pete. "One missed called from Grace and two voice mails from her."

Pete opened the phone. "How'd you figure the password?"

"Her birth date. Lucky guess. My niece said that's what she did."

Pete raised his eyebrows. "Kind of easy."

"Yeah."

Pete used her contact list to dial voicemail and then punched in the password. The first message from Grace played.

*"Hey Laura, just wondering if you wanted to hang out tonight, I know you've been a little down lately since all the stuff at school...well, anyway, me and Zack are just watching movies...if you want to maybe I could bring the movies over since my TV isn't that big. Okay, see ya later."*

"The missed call was in between the first and second message." Brad said. Pete nodded and waited for the second message to play.

*"Laura, it's Grace again. I hope I'm not bothering you but I'm kind of worried since this is my third call and you haven't called back. I'm not used to you not answering your phone...me and Zack are still watching movies...Um, I guess I'll see you tomorrow then. Bye."*

Pete exited voice mail and then pound the missed calls list and looked at the times. "All these were right when the murder was taking place." He said.

"Yep." Brad nodded.

"So unless Grace was standing over Laura's body calling her cell phone, it's a good alibi for Grace."

*The Yellow Note*

"Right." Brad glanced across the room and got a far off look in his eyes. "I think I need some coffee." He stood up from his desk and ran his hand through his blond hair.

Pete nodded and watched Brad strut through the open second floor. He stopped to flirt with one of the lady officers who was filling her coffee mug at the little beverage and snack area. She was relatively new and completely unfamiliar with Brad's tactics. The red head looked young too, probably naive. Hopefully, one of the other women would warn the unsuspecting gal. She was indeed the very reason Brad got up in the first place.

Pete sure appreciated the way Brad worked, glad to have him as a partner, but his lifestyle was something Pete had to choke down. There didn't seem to be a religious bone in the man's body and Pete had tried. Boy, had he tried. Up until recently, Pete made it his duty to try and insert a little bit of God wherever he could.

Finally, Brad left the blushing woman alone and walked down the wide stairwell.

Pete shook his head.

The phone rang. He stared at the blinking line 3 button for a moment before answering.

"This is Pete."

"Pete Monson?" A woman's voice.

"Yes."

"My name is Helen Orvitz. Did you not get my message?" She sounded arrogant and very irritated.

"Yes, I'm sorry, I did—"

"Why haven't you returned my call?" She said.

*The Yellow Note*

"I'm sorry about that mam, we're very busy down here and—"

"I thought you people were supposed to come and speak with all the neighbors about the situation to see if there were any witnesses. Aren't you concerned that I have may important information that may help you with your investigation?" Helen asked.

Pete bit his lip. He wanted to mouth off back to her. "We've been very busy, we haven't gotten to all the folks in the neighborhood yet. What kind of information do you have?"

"Well, I'd rather not discuss that over the phone, it may not be safe."

Pete rolled his eyes. He was going to try and reassure her that the phone was safe, but he didn't have the energy. "Would you like to come down here to the station? I can give you directions."

"That won't be necessary. I won't be driving down there myself. My husband is on business and he took the driver with him."

Oh, the snobby rich type. A bit like Kristine, Pete thought.

"Okay, then—"

"I was assuming you make house calls."

"We can arrange that. Can we come now?"

"That just won't do, see, my personal assistant will be here shortly to fix my nails. It will take about an hour."

Pete was waiting for her to set a time or *something*. After a strange, silent 10 seconds Pete finally said, "Will 4 o'clock work for you?"

*The Yellow Note*

"I supposed...I'll have to make the housekeeper aware of it."

"Okay then, we'll make it 4."

After Pete got her address, he set the phone down and lay his head on his arms on his desk. How could one person be any more difficult. The information she has had better be good.

The Orvitz's mansion was three stories high, dark gray stone with white trim and shutters. Pete drove up the freshly paved driveway, Brad sat next to him in the passenger seat , gawking at the structure.

"Oh man!" He said. "I thought the Thayer's place was mint, look at this thing. I can't wait to see inside."

"Hmm." Pete pulled his car up near the front door. Brad got out in a hurry, slamming the car door. Pete winced. His Lexus was only a year old, he hoped nothing got loose in the door. Pete finally got out too and they both walked up to the large front door where Brad insisted on ringing the old fashioned doorbell.

In a minute a tall dark haired woman wearing a starched, black uniform pulled the door open.

"You are the police I presume?" The woman spoke in a deep Russian accent. Must be the housekeeper.

"That's us." Brad said. He smiled widely at the woman who batted her eyelashes at him slightly.

"This way please." She held her hand out behind her and when Pete and Brad got into the wide foyer, she shut the door behind them.

*The Yellow Note*

"Wow." Brad said under his breath as they followed the housekeeper through the home. It was more like a castle than a home, only with lighter colors and a modern flare. There were huge paintings on the wall, enormous pieces of expensive looking artwork in the hallway.

At last the woman stopped in front of a set of French door which she opened. "Mrs. Orvitz, the police are here to see you." The woman waved her hand towards the room and Pete and Brad went in.

It was stocked with small palm trees, exotic flowers and even birds that flew around in the tall glassed room. A beautiful place that reminded Pete of the state zoo where he used to bring Heather when she was little. She'd loved the place, all the flowers and animals.

To the right was a patio of sorts with wrought iron chairs, a table and a woman with whitening blond hair that she wore in a tight bun. She appeared to be about 60, but perhaps older if she'd had face lifts. Pete assumed she had because her face was just as tight as her hair.

She didn't look up right away, just kept reading her magazine until she finished her paragraph then slowly put a book marker in it and stood up.

If she had any emotion Pete couldn't tell. Even when she got up next to them she only made a slight nod without a smile.

I'm Helen Orvitz." She said.

"Pete Monson."

"I'm Brad Cohan. How do you do mam?" He smiled as her.

*The Yellow Note*

Pete couldn't tell if he was mocking her or if he was just being Brad.

Helen simply blinked at him without expression. Brad's face turned five shades of red. Pete had to laugh inside. It was a rare thing when Brad got anything but a good response from a woman.

"I'll show you where I was." Helen said. "They followed her out of the greenhouse room through the long elegant hallway to the front living area.

"My husband Ken and I were having a glass of wine right here." She motioned her thin hand out towards the perfectly arranged room. "Ken was reading the paper there," She pointed to a brown leather chair, its back facing the picture window that looked over the front lawn.

"And I was here, writing notes for my article for a new magazine." She said. Pete nodded. So she was a writer, an author maybe. Maybe it was her article she'd been reading in the greenhouse room.

"I was having a thoughtful moment, looking out the window when I noticed a black sports car parked across the street." Helen sat down in an antique ottoman and faced the window.

"Just like this. I didn't think anything except that I had never seen that car before, at least not that I remembered. At just that moment, I could hear sirens. During the day we keep the windows shut and the central air on, but after dinner we usually turn it off and open the windows to let fresh air in, so I was able to hear the police cars. Otherwise we wouldn't have been able too." She cleared her throat and looked down at her pearl colored nails. She frowned

*The Yellow Note*

for a split second and Pete guessed she'd found an imperfection.

Pete glanced at Brad who looked sheepish still, but listening to Helen intently with his notepad in hand.

"Not ten seconds later I saw a figure run down the street to that sports car, get in and speed off. I expected to see the police behind the car, but eventually the sirens faded. Ken didn't hear a thing. I keep telling him to get fitted for a pair of hearing aids, but he doesn't think he needs them."

Helen got up from where she'd been sitting and straightened her blouse and slacks.

From where Pete stood, there wasn't much view of the street. Maybe a 30 foot section. Thick rose bushes blocked the rest of the street out.

"Were you able to see the person's face?" Pete asked.

"No." Helen said. "It was hard to see being that it was getting dark. But I do remember the car was a two door. Don't ask me the model because I don't know cars and even if I did I would have to be an expert to tell what brand it was."

"Male or female?" Pete said.

"Couldn't tell." Helen shook her head and crossed her arms.

"Approximate height?"

"I have no idea. Now, don't you think I would have told you these things if I knew them?" She tapped her foot twice on the hardwood floor.

"Just trying to do my job." Pete said a bit harshly.

*The Yellow Note*

"I see. I did just recall that this individual was wearing all black and a ski mask as well." Helen said.

"Anything else?"

"No." she said. "I'll show you to the door." Helen walked briskly through the living room to the front door. She opened it and waited.

"If you remember anything else—" Pete reached for a card in his pants pocket.

"I have your number I don't need a card." She said.

"Okay, thank you for your time Mrs. Orvitz." Pete nodded and Brad didn't say a word as they left the house. The door shut hard.

When they got to the car Brad threw himself into the passenger seat and slammed the door again. "What a piece!" He shouted.

"Yeah." Pete shook his head. "At least we got something. We'll have to find out how many people Laura knew with a black sports car." Pete could already think of one. Chloe Bennett's little black Ford Mustang. It made his lip curl. He wasn't sure if it was because he was mad at the girl or if it was what it would mean if they found out the sports car had been Chloe's.

# CHAPTER SEVEN

In the student parking lot of Raile High School Pete drove slowly up and down each row as Brad wrote down the license plate number of any black sports car they saw. So far there were eight, black, two door sports cars.

"Boy, look at that one." Brad pointed at a familiar Mustang. Chloe's. Pete wasn't going to tell Brad he knew whose it was. Actually, he felt uncomfortable not telling Brad. If he kept it a secret too long it might end up worse. Brad especially would wonder why Pete didn't share what he knew.

"Heather is friends with the girl who owns that car." Pete said.

"Really?" Brad kept staring at the car. "She must have some wealthy parents. Look at those chrome rims..the chrome detail…tinted windows. I'd have done anything for a car like that in high school."

"Her parents died awhile back." Pete said.

"Yeah? Inheritance then."

*The Yellow Note*

"I suppose." Pete wasn't really sure. He'd never asked Heather and it wasn't like he was going to ask Chloe about it.

"What does that mean?"

"Just that she isn't a very pleasant girl." To put it mildly. Pete came to the end of the last row and then headed towards the exit.

"I hope we come up with something from all these plates cause I really don't want to go asking the city for permission to view the security cameras at all the intersections. You know the rigmarole they always put us through."

"Right." Pete pulled out of the student lot feeling a little better that Brad didn't seem to care much about him knowing a girl from school who owned a black sports car. Maybe he shouldn't care as much either, it's not like there was proof that Chloe did anything, she was just...weird. It didn't mean she'd killed anyone.

Pete sat in his car, late afternoon, across from 1890 West Lake Street. The Hartson's place. It was a small house and every bit as trashy as the entire block. The yard was tiny, grass patchy and long, there were flowers under the windows, but mostly wild and completely overgrowing their old wooden buckets.

It was the kind of neighborhood that attracted all kinds of evil. During the day nothing extravagant happens, but when dusk fell, all the maniacs came out of hiding. Or else they woke up after having slept all day.

*The Yellow Note*

Once out of his vehicle Pete crossed the street, and took note of his surroundings. Especially, the black Sunfire in the driveway. It sat next to a beat up old Buick, olive green. The thing hardly looked drivable, but the tires were all inflated and the tabs were current.

As he passed the Pontiac, Pete peered inside and saw that there were a few boxes of what looked like party supplies in the back seat. Bright colored hats, streamers still in their packaging, birthday cake candles and sequins. In the passenger seat was a pair of blue and white pom-poms and white tennis shoes.

At the rickety old front door Pete peeked in through the screen and heard the sound of crashing and screaming and the occasional moan of a young voice. It made him reach for his gun, but then he realized it sounded like it was coming from the television.

Pete knocked on the door three times.

There was a footfall and then a thin leathery skinned woman wearing a black shirt and pants and a white, stained apron around her waist appeared at the screen.

"What do you want?" She said. Her voice was rough and no doubt why. The blond woman had a cigarette hanging out of the corner of her mouth. She didn't bother to use her hand to take a drag, just pursed her lips enough to create suction and inhaled.

"Detective Monson," Pete held up his badge for her to see. "Are you Brenda Hartson?" She nodded slightly. "We spoke on the phone earlier this morning."

*The Yellow Note*

For a second she just stared at him, her eyes narrowing.

"Well, come in then." She turned away from Pete, walked back in to the house and sat herself down at the counter on the other side of the kitchen. Pete opened the door and let himself in. The living area where he stood wasn't messy, but it looked dirty. The burnt orange carpet had cigarette holes in it, stains and lint balls in various places.

"Is Grace here now?" Pete asked. He expected her to be. He was on time and they'd made an appointment to meet at 11:00 a.m. Kristine had been a little sour about him working on a Saturday, but she was going to be at a woman's thing at church all day.

"Grace!" The woman shouted. Her voice cracked and she started hacking until finally she took the cigarette out of her mouth and set it down in an ash tray.

Pete moved farther into the house and saw Zack on the floor on his stomach playing a video game. He looked up at Pete for a split second and said, "Hi, Mr. Monson." Then went back to his virtual baseball game.

"You two know each other?" Brenda asked as she put the cigarette back in her mouth. She eyed Pete suspiciously.

"My son Steven is a friend of Zack's." Pete said. "They're in the same grade and basketball together."

Brenda didn't so much as nod, just kept sucking on her cigarette, sitting slouched in the stool next to the kitchen counter. It was pathetic that she didn't even know what her own son was up to.

*The Yellow Note*

Grace finally emerged from a room in the short hallway next to the kitchen. She closed the door behind her.

"Hi." She said. Her face was puffy like she'd been crying.

"Let's get on with this then." Brenda said. "I have to work in an hour. I don't understand why I have to be here anyhow. Gracie is a big girl, she can speak for herself."

"She's a minor." Pete explained.

Brenda shrugged.

"We can sit here." Grace cleaned a space for Pete on the stained sofa. He wasn't sure he really wanted to sit on it. Was it brown fabric or had it become brown? Pete sat.

Grace shoved some more stuff onto the floor and made room for herself at the opposite end of the sofa. She was wearing school sweat pants and a t-shirt.

"Turn that down a little Zack." She said to her brother. He nodded and pushed the volume down until the baseball noises were hardly audible.

"How long have you lived here?" Pete asked.

"Just since the beginning of summer. So about 4 months. Maybe a bit more." Grace glanced down at her fingernails. They were chewed on the corner and her bright red nail polish was chipping off.

"Where did you live before?"

"New York."

"Has it been hard, the move and all?" Pete wanted to get a feel for Grace as a person before he jumped into the serious questions.

*The Yellow Note*

"I don't know." She shrugged and looked up at him. "We've moved a lot so I'm used to it. We've just never lived this south before. And so many of the kids here have tons of money...their parents do. It didn't used to matter so much about that at my old school, but here it does a lot."

"The other students make fun." Pete said.

"No, I mean, I tried out for cheerleading at the beginning of the summer at the school and no one knew who I was and I have a fairly nice car so they just probably assumed I was upper middle class or something. I made friends with Laura right away and some of the other girls on the team too. By the time they realized that we didn't have money, we'd already been hanging out a lot and I guess they liked me anyway even though they always offer to drive in their more expensive cars. I never invite them over cause..." She didn't finish her sentence. Grace looked at her mom out of the corner of her eye.

"Did you buy the car yourself?" Pete asked.

"I saved up for three summers working. It's my first car."

"How have your friends been towards you since yesterday?"

"Still friendly. A few of the girls called me to talk and stuff, but I don't know if it will last or not."

"Grace, do you know why we wanted to talk with you?" Pete asked.

"I guess because I'm Laura's friend."

"And we ran some license plates on black sports cars. A witness said she saw a person with a black, two door sports car the night Laura was murdered

*The Yellow Note*

not to far from Laura's house. The car sped away just as police were arriving on scene. The witness said they thought it was suspicious."

Grace nodded with no change of expression.

"Is that your black Pontiac in the driveway?" He asked.

"Yeah." She nodded again.

"Do know anyone else with a black sports car?"

"I've seen kids get in and out of them, but no one personally, I don't know a whole lot of people yet, just the girls from cheerleading."

"Did Laura ever talk to you about getting notes at her house or in her locker? Threats or things like that."

"Actually, she did. She started getting them before I got here. She thought one of the gothic girls were doing it. I don't know what the notes said or how many she got, but I know she was really ticked about it."

"Who are the gothic girls?" Pete looked over at Brenda for a second. She was wiggling her crossed leg wildly, sighing every few minutes.

"Oh, just these girls that dresses in all black and stuff. Mainly it's just two of them. Laura hated them. I guess there was some kind of rivalry between her and her friends and them. I try not to be a part of it all, but since I'm friends with Laura's friends that means I'm part of it no matter what."

"Was Laura religious?"

For that question Grace raised her eyebrows. She looked like she was trying to figure out what to say.

*The Yellow Note*

"She talked like it, sometimes, but she partied and stuff like the rest of us. Laura told me that she believes in Jesus and that if a person didn't they would go to hell. She wasn't very nice when she said it. I think that's why her and the gothic girls have always had issues cause they like dark stuff, you know like satan, and Laura was the opposite...or something." Grace looked confused about it.

Pete nodded. "Do you know a girl named Chloe Bennett?"

"I know who she is."

"What can you tell me about her?"

"I don't really know her. I've talked to her like twice."

"Did her and Laura ever get into any fights or anything that you're aware of?"

"Oh yeah." Grace rolled her eyes. "Mostly yelling and stuff, but there were a few times when Chloe punched or slapped Laura."

"Did Laura ever press charges?"

"I don't know, maybe before I moved here. I think Laura was too scared to do anything major about it cause if Chloe went to jail or got community service or whatever, her friends would just be right there where she left off."

"Laura's father told me you were planning a birthday party for her."

"I was." She bit her lip and looked away. Tears were forming in her eyes. "I know the other girls would say that she was such a brat and everything, but she liked me, even though I was poor. I mean, why else would she have stayed friends with me after

*The Yellow Note*

she realized my family didn't have money? I couldn't give her anything. I didn't make her more popular. She had no weird reason for being my friend except that she liked to hang out with me."

"So I wanted to do something nice for her birthday. Her parents offered to pay for everything and even gave me money to go and get a bunch of party decorations. Most of the girls didn't really want to help out."

Grace hung her head low, shaking it as a few drops of tears fell to the ground. Brenda looked over at her daughter, eyes a bit sad, but she made no effort to comfort Grace.

"What about James Riley?" Pete asked. Grace wiped her eyes and her face turned red.

"What about him?"

"How well do you know him?"

"Um, pretty good I guess."

"He was Laura's boyfriend right?"

Zack turned his video game off and went to his room where he shut the door.

"Yeah, they were going out." Grace carefully rummaged through a pile of books on the sofa next to her and ripped a small piece of paper out of a notebook. She glanced up at Brenda who was lighting up another cigarette. Pete scrunched his nose. The air was already clouded up with thick smoke.

"Were they okay or did they argue a lot?" Pete watched as Grace found a pen and wrote something down on a piece of paper. She folded the paper and handed it to Pete, glancing at Brenda again. She wasn't looking.

*The Yellow Note*

"Uh, well, they fought towards the end here. But when I first met James he seemed like he really cared about her."

Pete nodded. He opened the paper and read her messy writing.

*I can talk about James, but not in front of my mom please.*

Confused, but honoring Grace's wishes, Pete looked her in the eyes and made a nod. "Then James didn't care about her all the sudden?"

"I think it was gradual."

"Can you tell me where you were Thursday after school, until you went to bed the same night?"

"I was here at the house with Zack. Mom was at work, so me and Zack hung out, ate pizza and watched movies till mom came home at like midnight or something. I called Laura on her cell phone a few times, she wouldn't answer. I was kind of worried cause she hadn't been at school all day. She had been kind of weird since Monday."

"Weird?"

"I guess since her and James broke up, I don't know." She shrugged and looked over at her mom. "The rest of the girls started to ignore her. I think James started some rumors or something to get her back for something she did."

Pete raised his eyebrows. "What did she do?"

"I'm not sure exactly, I heard that she wrecked his car and his school jacket and some homework or

*The Yellow Note*

something, I did hear a rumor that she spread about him being gay or something." Grace shrugged.

Brenda sighed from the counter.

"Okay, well, I think that's all for now." Pete stood up and looked at Brenda. She quickly grabbed a set of keys off the counter.

"Good," She said. "I have to get going." She took one more suck of her cigarette and made her move towards the door.

Pete followed her.

Grace followed him. Out the front door Brenda and Pete went, Brenda hurrying to her wreck of a car. She hoped in, started the loud engine and took off. Pete turned to the house as Brenda disappeared around the end of the block. Grace was standing right outside the door, waiting to talk to him.

"I'm sorry about the note." She said.

"What didn't you want to say in front of your mom?"

"It's about James. I was involved with James. Before Laura and him broke up. I know it was wrong, but a guy never showed interest in me before...not like him. I thought he was great, at first." She looked down at the ground. "He took advantage of me."

Pete raised his eyebrows. "You mean he raped you?"

"Um, we'd been fooling around...I don't know if you can call it rape, but I didn't want it to get that far. I'm so small compared to him."

"Grace, even if a person is married it's not right for a man to force himself on a woman. Did he hurt you?"

## The Yellow Note

"Not too much physically." She still wouldn't look up. "It was more emotional or mental than anything. I just wanted to tell you because I didn't know if he was like that to Laura or not. But what's done is done, I'm not going to get him in trouble or anything. I mean, I'm not pregnant or anything. And he hasn't done anything like that since anyway."

"Since?"

"After that little incident I tried to avoid him for awhile. He didn't talk to me either. But…I mean, he was nice enough yesterday to bring me home from school when I found out about Laura."

"Thank you for telling me Grace. I can understand why you wouldn't want to share that with your mother, but you should really talk to someone, at least file a report against him in case he does that to another girl."

"It wouldn't do any good. It was too long ago. I can't prove anything."

"Did you ever see him act violent with Laura?"

"She had a bruise on her face after school Monday. I assumed it was from him, but I don't know for sure. She wouldn't tell me. All she said was that her and James were over and she hated him."

Pete took a car out of his pocket and handed it to Grace. "If you remember anything, you can call that number."

"Okay."

*The Yellow Note*

"I just can't see Grace as a potential suspect." Brad said. He was rocking back and forth in his chair, his feet up on the edge of his desk.

"I agree...except this relationship she had with James. I don't know. I'm not sure what to say about it even. It's just strange." Pete said. He and Brad had been going over the details of the case, trying to put something solid together to work off of.

"Grace lived 900 miles away at the time Laura got her first note. You said she didn't even seem to have a grudge against Laura, right?"

"She was genuinely sad, I could tell that." Pete said. He sighed. "Unless she was trained by the FBI on how to lie."

"Ha." Brad chuckled.

"She does have an alibi, her brother. I didn't talk to him, but I'm sure she realized that we would eventually if we needed too. And she said it in front of her mom."

"James is suspicious enough. He was forceful with Grace and according to her, Laura had a bruise on her face that she suspected was from James when they broke up. So we should pay Mr. Riley a visit."

"Yeah, and I'd like to talk to Laura's teachers as well."

Brad let his feet fall off his desk and he reached for a file and threw it onto Pete's desk in front of him. "The examiner's report of Laura." Brad said.

Pete opened up the file and pulled the pictures out first. He quickly flipped through them and then pulled out the typed report.

*The Yellow Note*

"Nothing unusual." Pete said as he read through it. "Cause of death, blunt force trauma to the head… Mick suggests that the blue bottle found at the scene was what ultimately caused death. Did you talk to him?"

"After I read the report. It's in there, but he said that the bottom edge of the bottle matches the half moon in Laura's forehead."

"That must have been some thick bottle."

"You saw it. The lab measured it and found that the glass was 3-4 times thicker than the average water bottle. And I took a photo of the bottle around with me to some of the local gas stations. Jolly Mart down on 5th Avenue carries it." Brad reached to his left and held up a blue bottle, and exact match. Only this one had a label.

"Mountain Rush, Flavored water. Strawberry." Pete said. He leaned over and grabbed the bottle. It was open.

"Tastes great." Brad smiled like he was on a commercial. "I'm not much for that foo-foo type water, but that's good stuff."

"Almost eight bucks!" Pete said when he saw the price sticker on the top. "That's a racket."

"You're telling me." Brad nodded. "But, I think we're getting a feel for who this person is. Wealthy for one."

Pete looked down at one of the photos of Laura, then at the bottle of water sitting on the desk. He studied the close up of Laura's face. The mark certainly looked like it matched. "Whoever used that thing must have had some power behind their swing.

*The Yellow Note*

I don't even think a girl could swing that hard. Grace mentioned that James' was pretty big."

Brad raised his eyebrows. "Maybe I'll take a pop in at Laura's funeral." He said. "See who I can see."

"You're morbid." Pete said.

"What? Cause I like to see if I can find guilt in any of the sad faces in the crowd."

"I just know you."

"It certainly beats those CSI shows I used to watch as a kid, cause now I know how it really is."

"There weren't any prints on Laura's body." Pete said when he finished reading the report. He'd read it again more thoroughly later, but at least he had the basics rolling around in his head. He put the papers and the photos back into the file. "Being that the prints on the bottle were unmatched we should probably find some people to print."

"Mr. Thayer came in this morning to ask if there was anything he could do, and to see if he could get into his house for awhile to get some clothes and stuff. I asked him if he wouldn't mind getting printed and if we could get permission to get the Misses' prints." Brad said. "He didn't mind one bit. Said he'd do anything, so we ran him and her and they're not a match."

"I checked their house to see if there were any matching bottles. There were plastic ones, but no fancy blue one's like that." Pete told him.

"It wasn't Laura's prints, what about that Chloe chick?" Brad asked.

Right. Chloe. The mention of her name made Pete's lip curl. "Yeah, she's got a black sports car.

*The Yellow Note*

You know what I want to know, is how the prints were arranged on the bottle."

"Not in the report?" Brad grabbed the file. "I could have sworn I saw something about that."

"I want to see it for myself."

Down in the brightly lit lab Pete and Brad looked over the piece of evidence, examining it as they studied the oily prints now covered in dark gray dust that made it easy to see how the bottle was handled.

"They're all at the bottom here." Pete turned it over with his gloved hands and pointed to the obvious finger marks. "Like someone had been drinking out of it, but none at the neck of the bottle. If I was going to swing the bottle I would have grabbed the neck."

Brad nodded. Mick, the medical examiner, stood with them. "I was wondering about the same thing." He took the bottle from Pete and held it carefully by the mouth. "But if one were to hold the bottle in the way the prints are arranged, they could easily swing over hand rather than from the side or under, and connect with that spot of Laura's head." He pushed his glasses up on the bridge of his wide nose and blinked a few times.

"What do you think about the height of the suspect?" Brad asked. Mick put the bottle down on the stainless steal counter and crossed his arms as he thought.

"Because of the way the half moon lays, like a bowl on her skin, there are really two possibilities. The first, behind. A person of approximate height to

*The Yellow Note*

her would grab the bottle and swing down much like you would swing a hammer, only the hand would be around the glass like you would hold it to drink as you swung." He made the motion with his arm and as he grazed his ear, a piece of hair flipped over on his head revealing the bald spot that he probably desperately tried to cover every morning. Mick didn't seem to notice.

Brad glanced at Pete with a little smirk. Pete smirked too but felt bad. How he'd hate to be nearly bald. He ran his fingers through his own hair. Thank goodness he's not even seen much of a receding hair line.

"Or, if the suspect was taller," Mick changed his position and reached out in front of him. "They would swing much the same only they would have to be further away to get the same angle as the person who was shorter. What did the scene look like?" He asked.

"Messy." Pete answered. "There was stuff everywhere, it looked like whoever had been there fought with her a little while."

"Hmm." Mick nodded. "If the victim was already on the floor unconscious, a person of nearly any height would be able to get that angle with the bottle."

"What about force?"

"From the depth of the trauma underneath the skin, I'd say the suspect was a pretty hefty person, either that or they were completely crazed. I've seen some cases in which a child under the age of 12 was able to inflict more damage than a person twice their age. There's a point in the human body when

*The Yellow Note*

adrenaline has coursed through every part where one becomes so detached from reality, their capabilities are almost limitless."

# CHAPTER EIGHT

The Bennett house wasn't enormous, but it was certainly nice. It was a gated community much like Pete's only with smaller homes. They probably paid a fee to have their lawns taken care of, at least by the way things looked around here.

As Pete and Brad walked up the long sidewalk to the house, he checked the house number again. This was the right one. He just never expected Chloe to live in such a place. It suited her more to live downtown in some scummy neighborhood with screaming children and gangs and stray animals that roamed the street and mated with anything they could.

And now that he knew Chloe could probably afford an eight dollar water, he felt even more sure about her as his number one suspect.

Once at the front door, Pete pressed the doorbell and waited. There was movement behind the long etched glass window and finally the door opened.

Chloe?

*The Yellow Note*

On first impression the twenty-seven year old woman looked exactly like her younger sister, but when she smiled Pete realized it wasn't Chloe.

"Mara Bennett?" He asked, showing his badge.

"That's me." She said.

"Pete Monson. And this is Brad Carson. I spoke with you on the phone this morning."

"Right. Come on in." She nodded and waved them in. Pete stepped in and noticed a few pairs of shoes on a rug to the left.

"Should we take our shoes off?" Pete asked.

"Don't bother. I haven't vacuumed or anything yet today. Monday is always cleaning day. I usually get everything done before Chloe gets home from school, but I had to work this morning, so I didn't. You can sit in the living room and I'll get Chloe." She nodded to the right up into a large room that was set a few steps higher than the rest of the first floor.

"Actually, we'd like to have a few words with you before you get her." Brad said. Pete noticed the familiar look of attraction in his eyes.

"Oh, okay." Mara shrugged, seemingly unaware of Brad's wishful stare.

She led them up into the room and they all sat down around a glass coffee table. The place was immaculate. Why even bother cleaning? Maybe Mara was like Kristine in that they always had to have everything just right and if it wasn't, all heck broke out.

"I understand you lost your parents a few years ago." Pete said. Mara nodded, the half smile on her face fading.

*The Yellow Note*

"Yeah. It was a plane crash. It's been hard, but I know they're in heaven now. I'll see them again." She clenched her jaw and looked away.

"Has Chloe been able to deal with the loss as you have?"

Mara pursed her lips and sunk into her chair a little. "She's taken it harder. She's never been the most well behaved girl around, but since they died she's gotten worse."

"How so?"

"She's barely passing her classes, she gets into fights. Seems like she's always got a chip on her shoulder…" She paused and tipped her head to the right. "I'm sorry, wasn't this supposed to be about that murder?"

"It is." Pet told her. "We're just trying to get some background information."

"Because Chloe is a suspect." Mara's face turned cold.

"So far Ms. Bennett we don't have any clear suspects. We're just trying to talk to everyone who knew Laura Thayer, her friends, classmates, teachers and people who she didn't get along with."

"In other words, because Chloe is a certain way she's an easy target." She crossed her arms. Boy, things changed quickly around here. Maybe she was offended at Pete delving right into the subject.

"No. The purpose in any interview we conduct is to clear names, get any information that may be useful to the investigation. No one is guilty yet."

Mara seemed a little less tense after Pete's explanation, but her eyes were still suspicious. "After

*The Yellow Note*

you called, Chloe told me she was friends with your daughter Heather. Best friends actually."

Pete nodded. "They are."

"You wouldn't have other things on your agenda…would you? Cause you don't like Chloe hanging out with Heather."

"To be honest, I don't like that my daughter's behavior has changed since she and Chloe met, but that's not why I'm here. Beyond the fact that Chloe and Laura have been enemies, a witness said that they saw a black sports car near the Thayer's house at the time of the murder. It was a car the witness wasn't used to seeing and it was suspicious enough when the driver got in dressed from head to toe in black with a ski mask on and then sped away."

Mara wagged her foot up and down, looking from Brad to Pete. "Is that all you need from me then?" She clenched her jaw again. Pete had more questions but he knew he wouldn't get any thorough responses right now.

"So far I guess."

"I'll get Chloe then." She stood up and left the room.

"That was weird." Brad said quietly. He pulled at the neck of his shirt.

"I must have hit a raw nerve."

"I think she's hiding something."

"You're just upset because she didn't give you the time of day." Pete said. Brad's face turned red. He was just about to defend himself when Chloe came dragging in, her face drawn out and black make-up

*The Yellow Note*

caked on her eyes as usual. She was either stoned or had just woken up.

Mara followed Chloe in and both girls took a chair across from the guys. As it was every time, Pete felt the unease that came with being in the same room as Chloe. He shifted in his seat.

"Hi Chloe." He said, offering a smile. She didn't do a thing, just stared. "Did your sister explain why we're here?"

"Yessss." How fitting an answer for such a snaky girl.

"I can assure you we're just here to ask some questions, no one is a suspect yet." Pete said.

"Yeah, right." Chloe mumbled.

Anger came. Pete bit his tongue and glanced at Brad, hoping he'd take over.

"How well did you know Laura, Chloe?" Brad asked. Thank God he got the hint.

"Enough to know she's the biggest idiot I've ever met."

Mara raised her eyebrows at Chloe.

"You two have been in several fights, is that right?"

"She deserved to be slammed in the face." Chloe sighed.

"What was it that you two fought about."

"Our religious preferences."

"Can you explain?" Brad asked.

"Laura and her idiot self thought that I was a maggot under God's foot. She assumed she was O'Holy Princess…ha! So far from reality. She was a frickin' hypocrite."

*The Yellow Note*

Pete took note of Chloe's choice of words. Hypocrite. Mara looked horrified that her sister was being so blunt in front of two cops.

"How was she a hypocrite?"

"She liked to call her idiot self a Christian. But do you know how many times I've seen her falling down drunk at the beach? Or how about the steaming car windows and the hickeys on her neck she tried to cover with gobs of make-up. I thought Christians were supposed to look like Jesus, she looked like a frickin' devil dressed up in a cheerleading outfit."

Chloe spit the name of Jesus out of her mouth like it had a bad taste. It probably did to her.

Brad looked over at Pete, his eyes wide.

"Where were you last Thursday after school." Pete leaned forward, irritated. The girl was full of hate and rage and it grated on him. No wonder Heather had become the way she was.

"I don't know." Chloe shrugged. "Probably high, drunk, sleeping. Maybe I was out with friends. I don't keep track of dates and times just in case some detectives come barking up my tree."

Mara didn't seem to be shocked at Chloe mentioning getting high. It bothered Pete though. If she were getting high all the time, it was certain Heather was too.

"So you don't have an alibi." Pete said.

"No."

"You have a black Mustang, is that right?"

"Yup."

"Do you ever let your friends or family drive your car, say to be sober cab or just for a joy ride?"

*The Yellow Note*

"No one touches my car...except Heather. I'll let her drive. But no one else. Why are you asking me that?" Chloe glared at him.

"A witness said they saw a black sports car a few blocks from the Thayer's house Thursday night."

Chloe frowned. For the first time ever, Pete thought he saw a glimpse of anxiousness in her. It made his unease wane a little. Finally, the tables were turned, if not just for a moment.

"Where did you get the money for such an expensive ride?" Brad asked.

"My dead parents. Where else? I don't work and I don't sell drugs, in case you were wondering."

The Bennett's phone rang. Mara got up. "I'm expecting a call, I'll be right back." She said as she hurried out of the room to answer it.

Pete looked back at Chloe. Her eyes were locked in on him. A strange feeling suddenly entered the room.

"You're not so comfortable here with me are you Peter?" Chloe said. The tone of her voice and the smirk on her face was pure evil. "You're itchy in your own skin, you avoid God, even avoid the Bible these days don't you?"

Brad looked over at Pete.

"Too bad Peter." She shook her head and leaned forward quickly. It made him flinch. "You think God still protects you even if you don't spend time with Him? Sometimes you're so afraid of things...you're even afraid of me." She chuckled.

Was it her, or some demon from hell trying to steal his faith. Did he even have faith?

*The Yellow Note*

"You're so afraid right now you'd run for miles if it weren't for the massive pride you've got that makes you so concerned for what people think of you. You think you're so strong, that nothing can shake you because you've got God. But where's your faith?"

Pete clenched his jaw. He was breathing heavy now.

"Oh, did you think Kristine was the only one full of herself? Your family is so screwed up, you can't see up from down. You can't sleep, you can't think. You can't save anything now. Not your precious daughter, not your ignorant wife...I just hope nothing happens to your prized son Steve." Chloe stood up. Pete stood up. Brad stood up too, but backed away.

"It's too late." Chloe said.

"It's never too late." Pete said through his teeth.

"Do you really believe that Peter?" She took a step towards him. "You've spent so many years working late, ignoring your wife and forgetting your kids...they've all drifted away from you. Away from God. What kind of man are you? You've failed yourself, you've failed your family and you've failed God. You can't fix this one. I'd say good luck, cause you'll need it, but luck doesn't have anything to do with it now does it?"

She started leaving the room, but then stopped and turned to Brad. "And you, Just keep doing what you're doing. Hell awaits you." Suddenly Chloe's face changed. She blinked and looked completely confused. She whipped around and headed out.

As she left the room, Mara came in. "Are you guys done already?"

*The Yellow Note*

Both men, stunned, didn't answer at first.

"Ah, yes." Pete cleared his throat. "Thanks for your time. If there's anything else we'll be in contact."

Pete kept his foot heavy on the gas, his knuckles were turning white on the steering wheel. Neither he nor Brad has said a word since leaving the Bennett's house. Pete felt a little sick, mostly nervous and very angry.

"What the heck was that?" Brad finally asked. His face was still pale.

"That, was Chloe."

"I know you said you didn't like her hanging out with Heather, I guess I didn't realize...I thought you were just being a paranoid dad."

"We need to print her ASAP."

"I agree. She creeps me out." Brad shivered.

"We'll call her in and have one of the other guys do it." Pete said.

"I don't know if I believed in devils before, but I do now. I feel like going down to a church and doing some Hail Mary's or something."

"Hail Mary's won't help."

Brad turned to face him. "Doesn't look like what you're doing helps much either."

Pete grit his teeth.

Brad was right. Pete wouldn't admit it to him, but he was laden with fear. He wasn't sure what to do. If Jesus was on his side, why was he so afraid?

*The Yellow Note*

It was almost 7 p.m. by the time Pete finally left the station and went home. He'd have stayed later, but he'd not been able to concentrate since leaving the Bennett's. Brad had seemed like he'd gotten over it after about an hour and would probably still be buried in files, eating take-out at midnight tonight.

Besides the unfocused mind, Pete had a strange, rare urge to see if everything was okay at his house. It was probably Chloe's fault. She had his brain whirling with thoughts.

Heather's car was still in the garage when he got home and so was Kristine's. Everyone should be there. Pete shut the garage door and entered his house. It was quiet except for the clicking of heels. Kristine. She always wore heels. She came hurrying through the front hall and stopped short when she saw Pete taking off his shoes.

"Oh, you're home." She said. Her hair was done up and she was struggling to get a pair of earrings in. "There's dinner in the fridge. Steve already ate, Heather's in her room. She's still grounded from her car remember, so don't let her go anywhere. I have a client dinner meeting."

Pete set his shoes on the little mat next to Kristine's running shoes. He could tell he hadn't arranged them neatly enough when she gave him one of 'those' looks. He sighed, bent down and straightened his shoes. *How dumb.*

"Okay." He said.

"Dang it." Kristine mumbled, still trying to force the earring through. She turned to the wall and looked into the hanging mirror and at last pushed the silver

*The Yellow Note*

hoop through her ear. Pete used to help her with it when she had trouble herself. He used to do a lot of things. Somehow they'd become unusual now.

"I have to go. I'm running behind schedule." She stooped down to pick up her large portfolio bag and started for the door. Before he could say any more, she'd shut the door behind her and he heard her car start and the garage open.

It used to be that they'd say I love you before either of them parted ways. He'd almost said it. Why hadn't he? Pete's shoulders hung down. He did still love her...didn't he? Of course he did. But their relationship had taken on some sort of acquaintance tone to it. Strange. Almost as if they were just roommates living in the same house, but with separate lives. This wasn't what he'd envisioned for them as a young man. He knew it hadn't happened over night. It's just that he hadn't seen it happening at all.

Pete's stomach growled.

He left the back entry and took a right down the hall into the kitchen. He pulled open the stainless steel fridge and looked at its contents. A plate with pork chops, beans and mashed potatoes was sitting on the top shelf covered with plastic wrap. Pete took it out and put it into the microwave. He watched the plate turn on the wheel, round and round till the timer beeped.

Pete sat alone at the kitchen counter, his own chewing the only sound in the room. Lonely. That was how he felt. Not just tonight as he ate, but every day at work, at home, even at church. A feeling of being detached from his life. It made him nervous and he couldn't eat anymore.

*The Yellow Note*

After cleaning up, Pete went to his study and found his burgundy, leather bound Bible and sat down at his desk. This would make him feel better. He opened the good book up to Psalms and started reading at whatever random place he'd opened too. For a few minutes he read, trying to meditate on the meaning and get something out of what he was reading.

It only made him more frustrated that he couldn't concentrate and finally he slammed the book shut.

*Chloe and her stupid words!*

She bugged him so badly that he felt like screaming. Where did she come off saying that kind of garbage to him, making him feel like crap, judging him and his family. How dare she talk to him like that.

Pete shook his head. He had to do something, get his mind off of that silly little girl with demons.

He got up from his desk and went upstairs to Steve's room. Steve was playing on the computer, a game controller in his hand as he squinted and winced while the computer made noises. "Hi dad." He said without turning form the screen.

"Hi." Pete stepped further into the room and looked around. "New game?" He asked.

"Naw. Hockey. It's an old one. I was kind of bored. Finished my homework and Zack was going somewhere with his mom. He told me you were over at his house Saturday talking to his sister." Steve paused the game and looked over at Pete.

"I was. I had to interview her."

"About that girl who was killed?"

*The Yellow Note*

"Yeah." Pete noticed that Steve's dark blue colored walls were covered with sports posters. Mostly basketball which was his favorite. Pete hadn't gotten any of them for him. "Where did you get all the posters?"

"Lot's of places. Mom got me one for Christmas last year." Steve turned to look around at them all. "Sometimes they have fund raisers at school for games so I bought a few. If me and Zack ever hang out at the mall we always go to the store that has every sports poster on the planet. It's awesome." He smiled.

"How do you get to the mall?" He couldn't imagine Heather or Grace driving them around. And Kristine didn't have the time.

"We ride our bikes."

"Five miles?" Pete didn't know if he liked that or not. Especially since he didn't know how a person would get from their house to the mall without crossing a few major highways.

"It's not a big deal." Steve shrugged. "We take all the back roads so we don't have to cross the highway. And there's a walking bridge anyway."

Pete nodded. "Are there any games coming up?"

"We play Fairfield next week." Steve's eyes brightened. Pete then realized how long it had been since he'd watched Steve play any kind of sport.

"Good. I'd like to be there." Pete grinned. Steve looked hopeful but not too excited. "I'll let you get back to your game now."

*The Yellow Note*

Pete back tracked down the hall, passed the stairs and stopped at Heather's door. He could hear her music, gross thrashing and yelling and banging drums. He knocked. The music got quieter.

"What?" Heather's muffled voice.

"Can I come in?" Pete asked. He wouldn't dare open the door without asking. He might get slammed with a flying object upon entry. That happened once and never again.

"Fine."

Pete slowly opened the door in case he'd hear her wrong. Her room was a complete disaster. He knew it would be, but seeing what was behind the constantly closed door was enough to make him cringe. Her mostly black and dark clothing was scattered all over the floor and draped on furniture, papers and books were stacked on her dresser tops with empty soda cans, silverware, a bowl of old cereal and many other miscellaneous objects.

Kristine had long ago given up trying to get Heather to keep her room tidy. They had constantly fought about it until Kristine told Heather that if her room was going to be a mess, the least she could to was keep her door shut. The door remained shut at all times now.

Heather lay on her bed on her stomach, a notebook in front of her but closed and a pen in her hand. She looked up at him.

"What are you doing?" He asked, trying to make his voice sound as friendly as possible.

"Writing." She answered.

"Homework?"

*The Yellow Note*

"No. Poems."

Pete didn't know she wrote poems. He didn't know she wrote anything. Well, except for the evil notebook full of hideous things.

"How long have you been doing that?"

Heather looked like at him like he was completely dense. "Since I was like two."

"Oh." This wasn't going so well. Pete wasn't sure what he was even doing. Maybe trying to reconnect on some level.

"What do you want?" Heather asked.

"Uh, I guess just to come say hi."

She didn't say anything, just looked back down at her notebook cover that was heavily doodled upon.

"I guess I'll let you write then." Pete started walking away until Heather finally spoke.

"Chloe told me you practically accused her of murder." She said. He turned back to face her.

"I didn't. I had an interview with her like I did Grace Hartson, like I will with other people as well. We ask certain questions because we have to. We don't even have any suspects yet."

"That's not what she told me."

*She's a bratty little liar, that's why.* "I can't help what Chloe perceived. We never accused her of murder."

"I don't even know why you're bothering with the case. Laura wasn't a nice girl."

"It's my job Heather. And just because Laura wasn't a nice girl doesn't mean she doesn't deserve justice. All human life needs that."

*The Yellow Note*

"Hmmm." She obviously didn't agree. "I suppose you'll have to ask me a bunch of dumb questions then too."

"Do you have something to tell me?"

She rolled her eyes. "No dad."

"It may not be the wisest thing to be hanging around Chloe right now."

"See, you do think it." She scowled.

"I think she looks suspicious. She hated Laura, she has a black sports car and she has a record of violent behavior."

"This is totally whack." She shook her head. "You can't tell me who to hang out with."

Pete left the room. Defeated again.

# CHAPTER NINE

Being called down to the police station Tuesday afternoon made Don nervous enough and it didn't help that he had to drive through the worst part of the city to get there. The neighborhood looked more like the city dump than a place to live and the people all cased him out like they were ready to highjack his car and leave him for dead.

Finally, at the large, old brick building, Don pulled into the visitor parking lot and parked his car nearest the door. He didn't think anyone was dumb enough to try and steal a car right in front of the cop shop, but you never knew. He made sure to lock it and check to see if anything valuable was laying out in the open.

Inside it wasn't like he'd pictured. The first floor wasn't hopping with activity like television portrayed, and the place wasn't messy with papers and garbage like he expected either. Everything was nicely organized, offices behind etched glass windows lined the walls and the reception desk sat in the middle of the room. Two middle aged woman sat behind the

*The Yellow Note*

u-shaped counter where they answered phones and tended to other office type tasks.

There were signs hanging from the high ceiling that pointed in the direction of the restrooms, the interviewing rooms, the staff cafeteria and booking. Everything was done in turn of the century style to emulate what it may have looked like when the place was first built over a hundred years ago.

Don approached the front desk and waited for one of the women to get off the phone. One finally did. "Can I help you?" She asked.

"My name is Don Graham, Detective Monson called for me to come up here." He said.

"Oh, yes. I'll give him a buzz." She picked up the phone again and pressed a button. "Pete, Mr. Graham just arrived. Okay, I'll bring him there." She hung up and looked at Don. "Follow me." The dark haired woman came around the back of the desk and took Don to the left and under the sign that said Interviewing Rooms. She showed him to a small bare room with cream colored concrete walls and a short table with four chairs.

"You can have a seat, He'll be down in a minute."

"Thanks."

He didn't really want to sit down, but he did anyway. The molded plastic chair wasn't comfortable at all, probably a good thing for all of those secret keepers who lied more easily when they were comfortable. Besides the table and chairs, there wasn't a thing in the room except for a video camera up the right hand corner. It was covered with a plastic

*The Yellow Note*

bubble and Don noticed a red flashing light indicating that he was probably being recorded.

Don tried to find a position that didn't cut off his circulation in his legs, but nothing worked. Why was he so nervous? He certainly wasn't in trouble. What if they asked him about the notes? He couldn't fib. He'd have to tell them.

"Mr. Graham?" A tall man with dark blond hair stepped into the room. He was bulky too. Not fat, muscular. He wore a clip on name card that hung from his shirt pocket. Don stood and they shook hands.

"Pete Monson." He said as he closed the thick door and sat down. "I don't usually do interviews at residences...except that for this case it just hasn't worked out to get people down here. You're the first actually." Pete smiled for a moment. "You're new to Raile High school."

"Yes." Don nodded. "This will be my fifth week of teaching here."

"Bit of an adjustment transferring from Beckard."

"I'll say." Don chuckled. He wasn't feeling so odd now, Pete seemed like a nice man.

"Not too harsh I hope."

"It's not quite what I expected as far as the students. They're a lot more rough than I'm used to."

"I bet." Pete said. "Laura Thayer was one of your students."

"I had her for third hour."

"I know it's only been about a month for you, but if you could just tell me what kind of student she was, how she interacted with other classmates."

*The Yellow Note*

"The few papers I did see of hers were pretty well written, not exceptional, but not poor. She seemed to pay attention most of the time unless she got a text message or something...I don't even know why they allow cell phones in the school. I never saw her talk much to any of the other students who were in her clique. I got the feeling from the staff that she was a model student, but from the kid's, I heard a whole different story."

"Can you explain that?"

"You hear things as a teacher. They don't think you're listening or care, but all the students gossip about each other. Even the quiet ones. I get to hear it all. I heard many bad things about Laura, I'm not sure that I ever heard anything positive."

"What about her friends?"

"I can recall a few of them making not so nice remarks about Laura when she wasn't around."

"What about Grace Hartson?"

"I have her for class too. I can't remember her saying anything negative about Laura, but she's new this year. Maybe she hasn't had time to see what the other students see. Actually, Grace and Laura seemed to have been better friends with each other than with any of the other girls." Don said.

"Have you ever see Laura in a fight with any of her friends, verbal or physical?" Pete asked.

"Her boyfriend James, but I think that's it."

"When was this?"

"Last week, Monday I think."

"You witnessed this personally?"

"Yes."

*The Yellow Note*

"Tell me about it."

Don told him what he'd seen and heard. "I probably shouldn't have been snooping. I hope I'm not implicating anyone by what I'm saying."

"No. We are very thorough. No one is guilty yet. So you noticed a bruise on Laura's face a few days later when she'd gotten into a fight with some other girls."

"That's right."

"The same fight my daughter Heather and Chloe Bennett were involved with." Pete said. His face got a little tight around the eyes. So Heather was his daughter? Don hadn't yet had parent/teacher conferences and the last names kind of just slipped in one ear and out the other.

"Yes, that's the one. Laura had told me that everything was fine until James broke up with her. I don't know what happened exactly but I'm sure there were rumors started or something. She told me she wasn't going to come to school anymore."

"Was she at school the next day?"

"No. I guess I forgot until now."

"That next day was Thursday, the day she was murdered. Did you notice any of the other students missing from classes that day?"

Don took a moment to remember the classes. "No. I don't think so. I don't know for sure, but I'm almost positive all my students except for her came to class. We do keep record in a log book, in case you need to know for sure."

"Do you have James Riley in your class?"

149

*The Yellow Note*

"No, I see him in the halls now and then, but I don't remember if I saw him that day or not."

Pete nodded and looked down at a small notepad that he had in front of him. "Did you ever hear any of the students threaten Laura?"

"James. The day they broke up, like I said before. And Chloe Bennett once said something about her and Laura's fight not being the end of it. She said it right in front of me when I went out to stop them from fighting."

Again Pete nodded. "This time he closed his little notebook, handed Don a card and stood up. "Feel free to give us a call if there's anything else."

"Okay." Don stood.

Pete smiled quickly and left the room. Don stared at the card. *I can think of something right now, the notes in my end table.*


After the interview with the teacher, Pete's mind was reeling with the possibilities. There were two main suspects now...at least for him. James Riley and Chloe Bennett. He was hoping it was Chloe. Pete was finding it hard to remove himself from his own personal issues with her. If Chloe were arrested and charged, she wouldn't be around Heather anymore. Win, win. Catch the murderer, save his daughter from a destructive life with her best friend Chloe.

Pete desperately want to have a talk with James so he could clear the boy's name and look in on that demon possessed maniac that was Heather's best friend.

*The Yellow Note*

Back at the office Pete found out that the Thayer's security system had been tested for failure. There hadn't been any, nor had there been a breach to the internal computer.

"I suppose that suggests that whoever killed Laura had to have known the code to get in." Pete said. He was tapping his pen back and forth on his cluttered desk, thinking.

"Unless someone came home with her and was there the whole time." Brad said. He yawned and leaned back in his chair.

"And that would still mean they knew her." Which made Pete a tad irritated. If that were the case, it couldn't be Chloe. "It had to be someone she was on good terms with."

"Right." Brad nodded. "Who then? You said Grace had an alibi. It wouldn't have been James cause they'd broken up..." He pursed his lips and sighed, glancing around the room. He caught eyes with the new lady officer and winked at her. She smiled back.

"Maybe one of her other friends."

Pete groaned. "I *really* don't want to interview that whole cheerleading squad. I say we print them all and if any of them match the ones on the bottle, then we look into it. That will save us a whole lot of time — speaking of time." Pete glanced up at the clock on the wall. It was way past dinner. Kristine would be mad. He'd promised that he'd be home so they could eat as a family...whatever that meant.

*The Yellow Note*

Coming home late proved to be easier than Pete had thought. Steve was the only one around. He was sitting in the kitchen watching the small TV on the counter eating a bowl of chocolate ice cream with chocolate syrup flowing down the heap.

"Where's mom?" Pete asked him. He opened the refrigerator and searched for a plate of food with plastic wrap. There was none.

"At a friend's house." Steve answered. He kept watching some silly looking show that seemed too young for his age.

"What's she doing there?" Pete found a container with roast and potatoes and carrots. Why hadn't she made him a dish like usual?

"She was mad." Steve turned to him finally.

"At what?"

"You."

Pete took the food out and set it on the counter. "Cause I wasn't home for dinner."

"She was talking to herself the whole time we were waiting. We waited for almost an hour for you. Heather even came down for awhile but she left with her plate after fifteen minutes. Mom almost cried." Steve scooped some ice cream into his mouth. He had chocolate in the corner of his lips.

Pete felt his heart hurting. She almost cried? Because of him? Suddenly, Pete wasn't hungry anymore. He put the container back into the refrigerator.

"Steve?"

"Yeah."

## The Yellow Note

"Am I a bad person?" Pete leaned against the end of the counter. Steve wiped his mouth with the back of his hand and looked at Pete.

"No. But I think you should talk to mom. When you're not around I hear her talk to herself in the kitchen a lot. She gets pretty angry at you sometimes. Even though she's gone too, I think it's because you're gone and she's lonely, so she works more and goes to friends houses."

Steve's face turned really sad. He pushed his empty bowl towards the dishwasher on the counter. "Are you guys gonna get a divorce?"

Pete was shook by the question, but really, he had every reason to wonder. "No, Steve." He said. "Me and your mom are just…well, things are different. I want to fix it, but I don't really know how. I don't know if it can be fixed."

Steve got off of his stool and pushed it under the counter. "Jesus can fix anything." He said. He stood there for a few seconds just looking into Pete's eyes, then he smiled and walked out of the kitchen.

*Jesus can fix it.*

The first coherent thought that ran through Pete's head as he awoke to that familiar buzz of his alarm clock. He'd set it a little later than usual being that sleep just wouldn't come last night.

He'd heard the garage door open and close at around 11 o'clock last evening and then nothing. Kristine was still using the guest room downstairs.

*The Yellow Note*

He had wanted to talk to her, but he wasn't sure how to go about it, or even what to say.

Pete took his time showering, shaving and dressing. There was no way for him to know if she was home or not. He had to eat something and he couldn't crawl out the second story window to his car that was in the garage. He'd just have to swallow what was dished out whether it be silence or a torrent of harsh words.

Pete carefully walked downstairs, listening for voices. He didn't hear anything but the occasional tink of silverware hitting a dish. In the kitchen Pete found Steve at his regular spot at the counter, his small Bible open next to his bowl of Lucky Charms.

"I thought you left for work already." Steve said. A dribble of milk came out of his mouth and landed back in his bowl. He didn't seem to notice.

"Nope. I didn't sleep well last night." Pete opened the cupboard above the six burner gas range and found the bread. Then he heard the clacking of Kristine's stilettos. Maybe he could fit in the cupboard.

Pete stayed facing the counter. Kristine's walking stopped short then faded out of the kitchen. Pete turned to Steve who shrugged.

Boy, if that's how mad she was—

The clacking returned, entered the kitchen again and something was thrown in front of Pete. A small ziplock bag full of white powder. He picked up and examined it.

"What's this?" He asked.

"You're the cop, you tell me." Kristine said.

## The Yellow Note

Pete could see her out of the corner of his eye, arms crossed, face pinched. She was obviously waiting for him to say something. He took a closer look. He couldn't be sure, but it looked like cocaine.

"Where did you get this?" He finally faced his angry wife.

"Leslie found it in Heather's laundry yesterday afternoon." Kristine said.

"Who's Leslie?"

Both Steve and Kristine blinked at him, looking confused. "The housekeeper. Where have you been for the last two weeks?" Kristine answered.

"What was it doing in Heather's laundry?" Pete looked down at the bag. That was a lot. A lot of money. He felt really dumb. Of course, he knew what it was doing in Heather's laundry. She'd been using it. Probably with Chloe. *Where the heck did she get money for this?*

"Don't be ignorant Peter." Kristine scowled.

"Why didn't you tell me yesterday when she found it?"

"Hmm, let's see, I don't know," she tipped her head in a cocky manner. "Probably because you weren't home." She opened the refrigerator and pulled her breakfast out. A bottle full of strawberry flavored energy drink.

"You should have called." He was getting tense now.

"I didn't want to call."

"Why not?"

"You didn't come home for dinner. You're never home for dinner."

*The Yellow Note*

"Neither are you anymore."

"Why should I be!" She shook the drink wildly. Her face was red. Steve took his opportunity to exit the room. "I come home every day to an empty house." She said. "I have a daughter who's on drugs, a husband who doesn't like me anymore and a huge, elaborate mansion that I can't even enjoy anymore!"

"That's not my fault." Pete said shaking his head. It was his turn to cross his arms. He didn't feel like talking to her rationally anymore. Not if she was going to be a snob.

"You started this whole thing."

"What?" Pete clenched his teeth together.

"Don't *what* me Peter." She took a few steps closer towards him and stuck a long finger in his face. Pete noticed Heather standing in the kitchen door. "I'm going to make a point to have dinner ready at six sharp. If you're home great. If not, too bad."

Kristine turned and walked away quickly, hardly even glancing at Heather as she passed her. Heather then scurried away towards the front of the house. Pete snapped back to reality.

"Hey!" He ran through the house. "You get back here Heather!" the front door slammed. Pete could hear the banging of heavy metal. He yanked the door open just in time to see Chloe's car speeding away from the house. And there he was, standing on his front step, a bag of cocaine in his hand. The neighbor was staring. Pete realized he probably looked like a nut case. Right now, he couldn't have cared less.

*The Yellow Note*

At 4 o'clock in the afternoon, Pete lazily walked down the long and wide stair case at the Raile police department. Brad had already made it to the bottom, bounding like a rabbit all the way down.

"Did you meet a girl or something?" Pete mumbled. Normally, it would be almost comical, but he was still sour at what happened this morning.

"I think I did." Brad beamed.

"At a bar I'm sure."

"Where else." He chuckled.

"Nothing good comes out of a bar." Pete reached the last step. Brad's face was no longer smiley. Pete felt bad. "Sorry."

"What bit you in the rear today?"

"I don't even want to talk about it." Pete had debated bringing the cocaine into the station with him, but it would have just added more to the heap that was already happening. So he flushed it.

"You'd better get your mind off of it now cause we have work to do." Brad led the way back to one of the interviewing rooms where Mr. Riley and his son James sat waiting.

"Hello, Mr. Riley, James." Brad greeted them with a hand shake. Then Pete did. "I'm Brad Cohan, this is Pete Monson."

Kevin Riley was a weathered man with deeply, tanned skin, a buzz cut and perfectly fitted clothing. James was a bit larger than his father, but it was evident just watching them together that Kevin was in charge at all times.

"Let's just get down to business then shall we?" Kevin said. It bugged Pete. Brad glanced at him

*The Yellow Note*

with an amused look on his face. Kevin was probably appalled that his son had to be questioned in this manner at all. He was no doubt embarrassed.

"Fine then." Pete said. "You were dating Laura Thayer, is that right James?" Pete didn't bother looking at Kevin.

"That's right. Until I found out she was doing things like spreading rumors about me and wrecking things of mine." James said.

"What kinds of things?" Brad asked.

She told all my friends that I wouldn't sleep with her cause I was gay. She ruined my school jacket, and tore apart the upholstery in my Jeep." He shook his head.

"You broke up with her then, after you found these things out."

"Yes."

"Did you physically attack her or argue with her when you explained it was over?" Pete asked. James looked down then at his father was sitting rigid in his chair.

"Things got a little out of hand. She was being so bratty to me. I think I slapped her pretty hard." He said.

"You *think* you did, or you know you did?" Pete asked.

"I did."

"Did you ever say anything that may have made her feel threatened by you?"

Kevin cleared his throat and looked at Pete. "You told me on the phone I wouldn't need a lawyer for my son." He said. "I'm about ready to call him. This sounds like an accusation to me."

"We're just asking some simple questions Mr. Riley. James doesn't have to answer any of them, if he doesn't want to. But it's more beneficial to you both if everyone is up front right now, instead of later and us having to get search warrants and things of that nature." Brad explained.

Kevin nodded. "Very well then."

"I might have said something nasty to Laura." James said. "I was really mad at her right then and I didn't want to have anything to do with her anymore. It had actually been a long time coming, but this just pushed me over the edge."

"We're also trying to account for everyone Laura saw September 27th." Brad said. "Take us through a rundown of where you went after school that day."

"Right after school we had football practice and I was there till five o'clock. Then me and some of the guys grabbed a bite to eat and I dropped two of them off and came home about seven. I was at home all night after that." James said.

"You can vouch for that Mr. Riley?" Pete asked.

"Yes." He nodded.

"What would cause Laura to do all those destructive things to you?"

James looked away, then at his father who nodded towards Pete as if to say, go ahead, tell him. "I was with another girl over the summer. She found out about it I guess, I'm not even sure how. One of her friends must have talked or something."

"So you were the one who broke it off."

*The Yellow Note*

"I told her that I knew what she'd been doing and she got mad at me and told me she knew about me and Grace, then she blamed me for the whole thing, like Grace was innocent or something."

Kevin didn't look the least bit concerned about what his son had just said. Pete wondered if they'd had a 'spill the beans' conversation before they'd arrived.

"And that's when you slapped her."

James nodded. "She kept trying to get me to talk to her more after I told her we weren't a couple any more. She wouldn't leave me alone."

"Did Grace know about this?"

"I guess she found out. She'd been avoiding me for awhile, so I'm not sure how she found out. News travels fast at school."

"You and Grace still see each other?" Pete asked.

"No."

"When is the last time you and Grace spoke?"

"Last Friday morning. She didn't know about Laura. I told her. I brought her home from school."

"Were you aware that Grace was planning a birthday party for Laura?"

"I knew about it. I wasn't helping her or anything. That would have been kind of awkward."

"Did you see Grace at all last Thursday after school?"

"No."

"Were you ever aware of any threatening notes Laura had received?" Brad asked.

*The Yellow Note*

"She told me about some notes she'd gotten at her house and in her locker at school. I don't remember what they said. She never showed me. She assumed they were from one of those goth girls."

"Do you know how many notes she received?"

"No." James shook his head, sighed and looked down at his watch.

"Got somewhere to be?" Pete asked.

"I'm missing practice."

"We're finished anyway." Pete stood up. "If you remember anything else, you know where to reach us."

Kevin Riley nodded slightly and led James out of the room.

Grace was starring out the window again. This whole week she'd been daydreaming or thinking as she focused on what was beyond the glass. Don was sure she had Laura on her mind, the agonized look on her face gave it away.

Don knew that Grace had never been a straight A student, but since Monday her work had drastically changed. It was sloppy and poorly written. She'd obviously not been paying attention to the assignments.

When the bell rang for lunch, Don called her up to his desk. He waited until after all the students were out of the room before he spoke to her.

"Do you have anyone you can talk to Grace?" He asked. She shrugged.

*The Yellow Note*

"Not really. There's not much to say now anyway." She said. She wasn't wearing any make-up today, or any nice clothes. Her jeans looked old, her gauzy shirt wrinkled.

"I see you're not wearing your cheerleading outfit today like the other girls. Isn't there a game tonight?"

"I quit."

"Isn't that one of your favorite things to do?"

"It used to be…" She bit her lip and tears began to form in her eyes. "I just can't do it anymore. That was Laura's life. She was captain. Now one of the other girl's will take her spot and it's not the same. It's like none of them really cared about her or something." She sniffed. "They've all just moved on like she went off to another school or is on vacation or something. I never had a friend like her."

"Are you still friends with the girls that you two used to hang around with?"

"I guess."

"I know it's hard for you now Grace, but time will make it easier and especially if you have a girl-friend who you can talk to."

"They don't really like to talk about her."

Grace hugged her books against her chest tighter. Don could almost feel her heart break. It was awful. It was times like this he wished that he had a lady friend who could comfort her. He couldn't just invite Grace over. That would be extremely inappropriate and against school policy.

"What about your mom?" He said.

*The Yellow Note*

"I don't think she would know what to say. My mom isn't a very social person. And anyway, she works between 12 and 16 hours a day. I hardly ever see her or have time to sit down and talk to her. I'll manage Mr. Graham. It's just been hard this week coming back to school, seeing her locker and not seeing her in the halls." Her lip quivered.

"I'll pray for you Grace."

"Thanks." She smiled weakly and for once looked him in the eye before she turned and walked away.

With a picture of sad Grace being on his mind and in his prayers all day and through dinner, Don had forgotten the mail.

It wasn't until the 10 o'clock news that he realized that he'd completely spaced checking the mail box. So very unlike him. It was routine to grab it right as he got home each day. He got up from his favorite spot on the end of his sofa and went out onto his front steps for the mail.

Yellow.

Out of the corner of his eye he saw it. Don caught his breath. He ripped the little note off the nail and jumped back inside as quick as he could. Lock the door. Throw the mail down on the entry partition. Read the note.

*I WAS THINKING MAYBE WE*
*COULD TURN THESE NOTES*
*INTO A CONVERSATION OF*
*SORTS. I WRITE YOU, YOU*

### *WRITE BACK. IT IS YOUR*
### *JOB TO WRITE. IS IT NOT?*
### *OR ARE YOU TOO AFRAID?*

Don glanced at Brownie. She was sitting on her doggie mat, perfectly content. Surely, Don would have noticed the note on returning home from school. He wasn't that out to lunch today, was he?

"Write back huh?" He asked out loud.

Feeling bold, Don sat down on the sofa again, pulled a pad of paper and pen out of the end table drawer and thought. Afraid? Not right now. He could feel the grace of God.

*I wish I knew who you were so I could put*
*A face to these words...but I guess I'll just have*
*To ask first why you chose me to write to*
*And what the purpose is with these notes.*

Don folded the paper, ran outside again and punched his own note onto the little nail. His note was white. It would be obvious to the yellow note writer that he'd written back. Now all he had to do was wait.

# CHAPTER TEN

The week had been a long one. With the entire cheerleading team having been printed and giving no match and no lead to progress the investigation Pete was feeling frustrated and tired. The long nights were taking a toll. And he'd not made it to dinner at six once since Kristine's declaration in the kitchen. It seemed to seal her angry towards him even more.

Pete lay in bed Sunday morning, thinking, wishing he didn't have to get ready for church. It would do him well to get a few more hours of sleep, but that would be another red check mark on his chart from Kristine.

He quickly pushed himself out of bed and made his way to the kitchen. As he made himself breakfast he heard Kristine upstairs, yelling Heather's name and then the sound of her bedroom door being opened. Brave woman. The routine was the same every Sunday. Heather was still in bed, Kristine was trying to motivate her, an almost impossible task.

Steve was ready.

*The Yellow Note*

The boy sat at the counter, another box of high sugar cereal in front of him. This time it was a kind Pete had never hear of before. Pete stirred his non-sugar oatmeal with milk before putting it in to the microwave.

A few minutes later Heather came through the kitchen's double doors and opened the refrigerator. She was wearing a pair of black jeans, holes all over them and strings of fabric hanging at the frayed edges. Her black tank top was too tight and too short and wrinkled...and there was a sparkling little gem in her nose.

Pete frowned.

He and Kristine had specifically told her that she could not have any facial piercings until she was eighteen. He didn't have the energy to say anything so he just leaned on the counter and ate his over-cooked oatmeal.

Thirty seconds later Kristine came busting through those same kitchen doors, letting them swing wildly. She reached above Heather into the fridge and grabbed the orange juice. It didn't take her long to notice her daughter's attire.

"Are you wearing that?" She asked. Kristine stood in the middle of the kitchen, orange juice in hand.

"What's wrong with it?" Heather sighed and shut the fridge door. She never ate anything in the morning, but every Sunday she stared into the refrigerator and scanned the shelves. Pete wondered why she even bothered.

# The Yellow Note

"What *isn't* wrong with it." Kristine said. Pete groaned inside. Didn't she know when to just let things go?

"You're so out of it mom. I wear this outfit all the time. You've never said anything before."

"It's too short for one thing, and you look like you just pulled some material out of a trash can and slapped them onto your legs. Kristine finally got herself a glass out of the cupboard.

"At least I'm comfortable." Heather said. She crossed her arms. Kristine blinked but said nothing. Until she put the orange juice away. Steve got up, put his dishes in the dishwasher and left the room.

"You're sloppy Heather." Kristine said. "I don't think if you were going to meet Jesus at Church today you'd be wearing that."

"I really don't think he'd care mother. He isn't there anyway."

Kristine cocked her head. "What is that supposed to mean?"

"It means exactly what I said."

Kristine put her empty glass in the dishwasher and left the room, her heels clomped loudly as she went. Then they stopped in the hallway.

"Heather!"

A grin crept onto Heather's face. Pete frowned. "What did you do?" He asked.

"I just moved that little red vase a little off center on the table, that's all." She shuffled her feet as she left the kitchen.

Just then Pete realized he hadn't talked to her about that bag of cocaine that had been in her laundry.

*The Yellow Note*

No use now. It would just cause a blow out argument and that wasn't something he wanted to do just before church.

Pete squinted across the large foyer at the church. Don Graham? He put a hand over his eyebrows to cut the glare from the bright over head lights beaming down on him. The teacher weaved through the mass of people slowly, a smile on his face as he nodded at folks he knew. He was inching in Pete's direction. It would probably be another minute or so before he got close enough so that Pete could say something to him.

As was her custom Sunday after every service, Kristine rambled on and on with her friends somewhere in the church sanctuary, lost among the nearly 2,000 members at The Lord's Fellowship Church. Today she would probably talk longer considering her irritation with him.

Steve knew the drill so took the opportunity to hang out with his friends in the church's full sized gymnasium. Heather would be out in the car listening to music on her IPOD or sleeping in the back seat. And Pete would wait.

Now and then he'd have a chat with Pastor if he wasn't busy or converse with acquaintances. But today he just stood in the foyer, hands in his pockets, watching the people that surrounded him.

Finally, Don got close enough to him and Pete stepped out to make himself seen. When Don saw and

*The Yellow Note*

recognized him he smiled wider and aimed through the crowd to Pete.

"Detective Monson, right?" Don asked. They shook hands.

"Pete."

"Okay, Pete. I didn't realize you came to church here. But I suppose it's such a large place."

"Yeah." Pete nodded. Out of the work setting he wasn't that great of a conversationalist. "I'm not here every Sunday though, work you know."

"Oh, right. When duty calls you got to be there."

"Yup."

"Family?"

"Somewhere." Pete chuckled. "They like to wander off. My wife's name is Kristine. I have a son, Steve who's fifteen, and Heather, you have her in class."

Don tilted his head. "Heather? Oh!" he nodded. "I guess I should have put two and two together, your last name and all. Wow, small world huh?"

"Yeah."

"How's the investigation going?"

"As well as can be expected. We don't really have any solid leads yet, a few things on the table, but nothing strong."

"Well, hang in there. God's on your side, and I'll be praying for you guys. Good to know a believer is in the midst of all this. It will turn around."

"Right." Pete nodded.

"I've got a pooch at home who's been cooped up all day, so I'd better run. It was nice to see you again Pete."

*The Yellow Note*

"You too."

Don left Pete in the foyer. Happy people surrounded him. At least they looked happy. Gleeful smiles were plastered on their faces, laughing and sparkling eyes and hugs. Pete didn't feel a part of all this. He was lonely, even with everyone around. He felt stuffed up inside, he needed air.

Pete tugged at his tie and made his way towards the front door. He had to push his way through the sea of bodies, nudging his way past stubborn feet that wouldn't move. He was getting very warm. Someone tapped him on the shoulder. He didn't stop. He couldn't. Pete hurried to get beyond the trap he was in, shoving people out of the way and finally making it to the door. He leapt up the stairs and swung the door open and stepped into the air.

Nothing but the sound of the freeway and a few birds filled his ears. At last, he was out. Pete wiped the sweat beads that had formed on his face and looked around. What was wrong with him?

After taking a few deep breaths, Pete began the trek through the large parking lot, passing car after car and finally seeing his own at the end of the sixth row. The spot he usually took.

He saw Heather's head leaned up against the back window. He couldn't tell if she was sleeping or listening to music. Now was a good time to have a little talk about the drugs from her laundry. Kristine would be a good fifteen minutes longer, plenty of time to discuss the matter. And Heather was stuck in the car.

Pete opened the driver's side door, got in and set the child safety lock to on. When Heather heard the click on all the doors, she opened her eyes and looked at Pete in the rearview mirror. For once Pete felt like he was in control.

"I don't know what you've been up to lately and frankly, it doesn't really matter. But it's going to stop." He starred right back at her. She averted her eyes. "I still have that bag of what I assume is cocaine which means I have your prints all over the plastic. Just because I'm your father doesn't mean you can take the liberty of doing as you please. And even though it would be hard for me to arrest you, I would still do it." He was lying about the cocaine and he knew he shouldn't, but it got the point across.

He watched Heather's red face twitch.

"I suggest you limit your contact with Chloe for awhile unless you want to get tangled up in this investigation."

"Why, cause you guys think she's guilty, even though you have no proof." Heather said.

"Because she's a suspect Heather, and you're her friend. It doesn't look good on you to be with her."

"That's all you and mom care about, looks. How we appear at church or wherever. It's so dumb." She shook her head.

Pete was finding himself surprisingly calm. "Maybe you're right. Maybe we do care more about how the family looks than we should, but you know what, I don't think I want to care anymore. I think I'm tired of that. I can't speak for mom, but I'm just

*The Yellow Note*

so done trying to keep up this act." He shrugged. And he meant every word he said.

Heather looked at him wide eyed and silent. He turned away and looked out the window, leaning his head against his seat. He didn't have any more to say.

Pete Monson was on Don's mind Monday morning as he prepared for the day at school. At the moment he was preoccupied with trying to find his little Bible in his desk. Finally, Don sat back in his chair as thoughts of Pete kept coming to him.

For a few minutes Don prayed for Pete, not knowing exactly what to bring before God, but saying everything he could think of. Then he was in search of the Bible again.

It wasn't where it should be.

Don riffled through his bottom desk drawer, pushing things aside and then finally taking everything out and putting it back into the drawer. He did the same to the other four drawers. When the search produced nothing, he sat in his chair retracing the last time he'd used the little black, leather bound Bible.

Just Friday he'd used it during lunch. He distinctly remembered putting it back where he always kept it, but yet it was no where to be found.

It wasn't that big of a deal except that he wondered who would have stolen a Bible. Who even cared? And when would anyone have even had a chance to come and get it? They would have had to know that he had one, know exactly where it was and make sure no one was around to see them steal it.

No matter.

*The Yellow Note*

Whoever wanted a Bible that bad must need one. Don would just get another one.

When Pete walked into work Monday morning, he found his boss Frank talking with Brad. Brad was on time? Pete set his keys down on his desk.

"Hey Frank, what's going on?" He said. It was odd Frank being here this early too. The man usually waited until around nine or ten to come in.

"I asked Brad to come in early this morning so I could get the low down on the case so far." Frank said. He hoisted his pants up over his larger gut. His eyes weren't completely truthful.

Pete shifted his weight from one foot to the other and looked at Brad. Frank almost never talked to them about a case, unless it was really complex.

"Ah, okay." Pete said. Brad had a strange look on his face. He turned away from Pete.

"I'm going to have you guys print another handful of people. I know you already did the cheerleading squad including Grace, but here it is." Frank picked up a piece of paper and handed it to Pete.

Pete read the first few names, students that knew Laura, then it was Chloe Bennett, James Riley, Heather Monson. Pete recoiled and looked at his daughter's name last on the list.

"If these all come clean, then we'll look into some other areas, perhaps interviewing the whole cheerleading squad individually." Frank said. "I didn't realize that you guys had such solid prints available from that bottle."

*The Yellow Note*

There was a moment of awkward silence.

"I feel out of the loop here." Pete said. "Why is Heather's name on this list?"

"I went to Frank, Pete." Brad told him. "I didn't know how you would react so I figured I'd get some back up."

"Back up? But she's not ever a suspect."

"Neither were the girls on the cheerleading team." Brad said. "But we printed them."

"She's had conflict with Laura. Gives us reason to." Frank said.

Pete rolled his eyes. He couldn't believe what he was hearing.

"Well, I guess that's my cue." Frank said. He turned on his heel and left to talk to some other co-workers across the open room.

Pete looked back at Brad.

"I'm sorry buddy. I really didn't know what to do, I've been thinking of it the past few days." Brad said.

"You could have talked to me first." Pete plopped down at his desk chair.

"Just for the record, I don't think Heather is involved, but we have to explore every angle. That's our job."

*I know the stupid job!* Pete thought.

"Well you must think something if you want to have her printed. We don't just bring random people in and tell them they were picked out of a hat."

"She's Chloe's friend."

"So?"

*The Yellow Note*

"Frank was concerned about you anyway Pete." Brad leaned across his desk and spoke quietly.

"Concerned about what?"

"How you've been."

"How I've been? He hardly ever sees me. Why would he be concerned?"

"It's not like he works at another office. He sees you walk by through the day, hears stuff from the other guys...you know how things are around here."

Oh, Pete knew alright. He didn't like it.

"Well, I'm fine. And if he was so worried he should have come to me." Pete tried to find a pencil and a pad of paper on his desk. He found the paper, but no pencil. He wanted to have something to do with his hands so he didn't have to look at Brad.

"He asked me if you should be taken off the case." Brad said. Pete looked at him. Was he on Frank's side?

"What?!" Pete almost yelled. A few of the other people in the room looked over at him. "Why? I haven't done anything illegal and I haven't been sloppy with the work. Frank knows he can count on me...on us. We're a team. No one works better together than we do. It hasn't even been two weeks yet."

Pete could feel all the muscles in his whole body tensing up.

"I told him I didn't think you should be taken off, but he told me to watch you." Brad said.

"What was his reasoning?"

"Mainly that Heather is friends with Chloe and you might be biased."

*The Yellow Note*

"I can't stand Chloe. I wish she were in jail right now."

"Point proven."

Pete let his jaw hang open. "I can't believe this."

"You could use the family time Pete. Frank's not the only one who notices."

"I'm not going anywhere, I'm not being thrown off the case. I'm going to do my job, unbiased. You hear me? And for your information I'd go stir crazy if I were at home all day long." Pete crossed his arms.

Brad smiled. "Now that's what I like to see."

"And I still think Chloe is guilty." Pete said.

"I'm betting on James." Brad chuckled.

"Betting?"

"You want in? A few of the other guys are in on it."

"I don't bet."

"Sorry, I forgot."

"But if I did, I'd put in $100 on Chloe."

Brad laughed again. "I'll mark you down for $100, course you can't take the pot if you win."

"I know." Pete let himself grin. He hadn't smiled in a long time.

The final bell had rung at Raile High school Monday afternoon. Don leaned back in his chair behind his desk and closed his eyes. Earlier in the day he'd asked Chloe to see him after school was done so they could talk about her grades. He wondered if she'd even show up. He wasn't counting on it.

But if she didn't, he'd be having a word with her sister. Don really didn't want to get her involved so he prayed Chloe would take a step away from being irresponsible and show up.

The sound of shuffling shoes.

They stopped. Don opened up his eyes. There stood Chloe, empty handed, dressed in black and sporting those clompy combat boots that seemed to be her favorite.

"Hi Chloe, why don't you pull up a chair." Don said. He sat up in his chair. Chloe looked over at the little green plastic chair near the door.

"Do I have to? I mean, it won't be long will it?"

"As long as it takes."

"I'll stand." She crossed her arms and starred at him, waiting. He really wished she'd sit down.

"I've been meaning to talk with you about your homework." He looked down at the pile of crinkled, half written or poorly drafted assignments. "Do you have enough time to get all your work done after school?"

"I guess." She shrugged and sighed.

"I know that every student has at least one class of study hall a day. Is that something you take advantage of?"

"I do my other classes homework during study hall."

Don nodded. He knew she was lying but there was no use trying to argue with her about it. And he'd also talked to her other teachers and they confirmed her below average grades.

*The Yellow Note*

"You're a bright girl Chloe, I know that sounds cliché, but I'm serious. The topics you choose to write on are risky, which is a good thing, and your vocabulary is well rounded, but the effort you put in to doing even an average job just isn't there." He studied her face. "The piece you did on your parents was great, you put me right there at their funeral and the emotion I could feel, it was really good. It could have been perfect. You left it at first draft stage. Did you even complete the three drafts I asked for?"

Chloe looked down at the ground and shook her head. "Not really."

Don was surprised at her change of attitude. Her normally hard exterior wasn't there so much right now. He wondered if it was because of the subject.

"Do you miss them?" He asked.

"I've learned to deal." She said, still looking at the floor.

"It's okay to be sad about them Chloe. It's normal to grieve for awhile."

Suddenly, her face turned red and angry and she looked up at him with eyes so full of hatred he felt chilled.

"God killed them. He hates me, so he killed them. They thought they were doing the right thing by following Jesus, but now they're dead."

Her crossed arms were so tight across her that Don thought she might break a rib. "I hate Him cause he took them and he left us to suffer and live hell on earth until we die too. And then he expects us to give our lives to him and do what the Bible says. Then he kills us too."

Oh boy.

The devil had twisted this girls mind up so bad. It made Don mad, not at her, but at the lies she'd been fed by the enemy.

"God did not kill your parents Chloe." He said firmly. She blinked. It was almost as if the words slapped her in the face, causing her to be speechless. "God is a good person. Satan is the one who steals, kills and destroys. And he's been lying to you so that you get angry with God and live a depressed life without joy. Satan doesn't care about you. He's the one who want to kill you."

"Ahh!" Chloe yelled. She slammed her fists into his desk, knocking over a pen holder. "You don't know what you're talking about!" She swiped her papers off his desk and on to the floor.

"You can't make me mad at you Chloe." Don stood up and faced her. "Jesus told me to love, and that's what I'm going to do."

"Love? Ha! I don't care. Not about school, about you or about anyone." She breathed through her teeth. Don noticed sweat beads forming on her forehead. It was obvious the fight she had going on inside of her. Good versus evil. He'd seen it enough to know, just not so close before.

Chloe reached up to wipe her face and when she did Don saw the scars on her left wrist. There had to be at least ten. Some old and white, some more recent, still red. His heart felt like it was being squeezed hard. She evidently didn't even care about herself.

*The Yellow Note*

Chloe's lip quivered and for the first time Don saw softness in her. But she quickly turned away and left his room. So much for the teacher/student conference.

Don was enjoying his nightly devotions on the sofa when Brownie lifted her head. Her eyes were locked on the front door. Then there was a clank. Brownie jumped up and ran to the door barking. Don put a bookmark in his Bible and got up too. Brownie's hair was standing on end.

After flipping the outside light on, Don peered out the peep hole into the dark neighborhood. Brownie was still barking.

"Shhh!" Don said. "Quiet." Brownie sat down and whined a few times but her body was still tense, paws moving back and forth.

Out of the peep hole Don could see just the corner of a piece of yellow paper. He unlocked the dead bolt and tanked the door open. Another note. He scanned the street. Suddenly, a shadow darted across the neighbor's yards, making other dogs bark. The shadow hurdled one chain link fence and then disappeared into a back yard about five houses down.

Don pulled the paper off the nail and went inside to read it. Brownie followed him to the sofa where she sat and put her chin on his leg.

***IN RESPONSE TO YOUR QUESTION***
***IT'S NOT WHO I AM THAT'S THE POINT***
***IT DOESN'T REALLY MATTER WHO I***

*The Yellow Note*

*AM, IT MATTERS WHO YOU ARE. ALL
THE OTHERS FAILED SO FAR. YOU'RE
THE MOST ACURRATE SPECIMEN OF
CHRISTIANITY I'VE SEEN YET.
WHAT DO YOU LIKE TO DO FOR FUN?
I LIKE TO WATCH PEOPLE.*

The fear tried to creep in as it did with every new note he'd received, but Don wouldn't let it get a hold of him. This was by far the longest one and this time, Don actually felt himself intrigued.

He pulled out his own paper and pen from the end table and began to write.

*I'm curious, are you the same person who put a note at the*

*Thayer's house? The thought is a bit disconcerting.*

Don stopped and looked at what he'd just written. He didn't know if he wanted to be that honest with the mystery writer, but maybe it would make the person more comfortable with him and give him a little more information.

He continued.

*What do I do for fun? I guess I'm really a homebody and I don't do much. I like to take my dog for walks. Would you tell me if I've seen you before?*

Don folded the note once, went to the front step and posted it on the nail. He then looked around to see if he could see anything. Nothing. But he was

*The Yellow Note*

sure the note writer was watching. He could feel their eyes.

# CHAPTER ELEVEN

"You think I did it." Heather mumbled. She examined her finger tips, blackened by printing ink.

Tuesday afternoon the seven students on the list were summoned to the police station to have their prints taken. "I don't know how many times you've said that since we left." Pete said. He was driving her home now. He felt like a jerk, but what else could he do? It was his job, and he certainly didn't want to be taken off the case.

He merged right and took the exit ramp that would take him to their neighborhood. "I told you that because you're friend with Chloe, things might get weird. Remember that? We were in the parking lot at church, just two days ago. I warned you. You should be happy because when your name is cleared you don't have to worry about anything."

Heather sighed and shook her head.

Pete glanced over at her and saw a tear rolling down her cheek. She quickly turned away from him and stared out the window.

*The Yellow Note*

"You're crying."

"Good observation dad." She sniffed.

"Why?"

"Why do you care?"

Pete pursed his lips. Fine he'd just shut up then. No. Not anymore. He slammed on the brakes, swerved the car to the curb and came to a stop. Other cars honked, someone even flipped him the finger.

Heather, who wasn't wearing a seat belt, braced herself against the dash board. "Are you crazy!" She yelled.

"No, I love you." He shoved the car into park and leaned towards her and touched her arm. "I care why you're crying because I love you. I know I've been a passive father most of the time and I'm not around much—"

"Not around much?" Heather rolled her eyes and pulled her arm away. "It's been years since you were home much. You and mom suck. Neither of you know how to be parents. Mom's so stressed out and busy at work that she's starting to look old, you treat her like she doesn't even exist. I couldn't imagine being married to a guy like you. I'd leave."

Ouch.

Pete cringed and prepared himself for more because it didn't look like she was finished with him yet.

"And you just let her walk all over you. Be a man and put your foot down."

Oofda.

Pete was ashamed of himself. Everything she said was true. He felt overwhelmed with it all. "I'm sorry Heather."

"Sorry doesn't help anymore." She said.

"Then what?"

"Change. Duh." She pushed the door open and got out of the car.

"Where are you going?"

"You want me to stay in the car until you pull into the garage?" She motioned across the street with her head. Their house. Heather shut the door and ran across the street, up the lawn and into the house.

Boy, was he out of it. Pete felt more like the child than the adult here right now. Perhaps it would be best if he just sat and thought for awhile

At 6 o'clock sharp, just as it had been since Kristine made her declaration, dinner was served. Pete hadn't made one of them on time. Tonight however, he had to. No, he wanted too. He wasn't quite sure how to change, but maybe being at dinner would be a start.

It was pretty quiet while everyone ate, Kristine making small conversation with Steve, who was always animated and lively when he was talking. Then it died down again until Pete caught Heather watching him with her sneaky little eyes. He didn't have a clue what she was thinking, but it didn't look nice.

Finally, she set her fork down, wiped her face with the cloth napkin and spoke. "Dad has something

*The Yellow Note*

pretty interesting to share, don't you." She glared at him.

"Oh?" Kristine looked over at Pete, her eyes no more kind than Heather's. Steve looked too. Pete felt his face heating up. They'd all stone him for sure.

"I don't know if interesting is the word Heather." Pete said. He chuckled lightly, hoping the stones he'd get hit with would be small.

"What is it?" Steve asked. His face was eager and ready to listen. To him it was probably something exciting.

"If you're not going to tell them, I will." Heather said. Before Pete had a chance to say anything, she looked at her mother and Steve and launched the dreaded news. "Today, after school, dad dragged me down to the police station and had me printed." She paused.

Kristine's mouth nearly hit the floor.

"Cool!" Steve said. "You got to see the booking room then."

"I sure did." Heather eyed Pete. She was going to make a show of the whole thing. He sighed and resigned himself to the fact that she wouldn't stop until she'd said it all. "Supposedly, there is a piece of evidence in dad's murder case that has prints on it and they're trying to match them. And since my friend Chloe is a suspect, I guess that means I am somehow related."

"Really?" Steve looked confused.

"Peter," Kristine looked at him. "Chloe is a suspect? Why didn't you tell me?"

"Because I—"

*The Yellow Note*

"And you printed Heather?" She gasped looking horrified. Pete wanted to hide.

"You could have just taken my prints off that bag of cocaine you found anyway, like you said."

Heather stood up and looked down at her plate of un-eaten food. "You and mom should sit here and have a long drawn out yelling match now, call each other losers and be done with it." She stood there. Steve looked like he felt awkward. Kristine had her fork midway between her plate and mouth, a piece of steak ready to be eaten on its end.

"Come on, I'm waiting." Heather said.

"What are you doing?" Pete asked.

"Everything that happens around here just turns into the stupidest argument, so I'm just helping you get over it quickly so I can go to bed and not have to listen to it."

Kristine shut her mouth and set her fork down. For once she was speechless.

"Give me your phone." Pete told Heather. He held out his hand.

"Why?" She crossed her arms.

"You told me to start putting my foot down. Chloe is a bad influence on you, and I see how many minutes you spend on your cell phone talking to her when the bill comes every month. Hand it over." He demanded.

"You can't do that!" Her face turned pale.

"Yes I can." He stood up. "And I'm going to right now. And just so we're clear, you're grounded from your car until I think you're ready for responsibility."

*The Yellow Note*

"Responsibility!" Heather yelled. "I'm more responsible than you!"

"If that's the case, then it changes right now. Give me your phone."

Heather stomped her foot in protest, but ripped the phone from her back pocket and was about to hand it to him but dropped it on the table. Then after her face turned bright red with anger she took her plate, raised it up and threw it across the room. It dented the wall and food flew everywhere.

"You suck!" Heather screamed and ran from the kitchen. Pete heard the stairs thumping and then the slam of her door.

Steve looked like he was about to cry. "Can I be excused?" He looked at Kristine. She stared at him blankly.

"Go ahead Steve." Pete said. "You can leave your plate here. I'll take care of it."

Steve stood up and left.

Pete walked over to the mess Heather had made and began cleaning it up. When he finished, he set the broken plate on the table with the pieces of food. Kristine was just sitting there, looking forlorn.

"Kris, I want to—"

"Don't!" She put up her hand towards him. "Don't talk to me. I can't believe you. It's like every day you get a little more distant, now I don't even know you." She got up, her hands shaking. "She's our daughter Peter, she's not guilty." Slowly, her body moving carefully, Kristine left the dining room. He could hear her whimpering as she went downstairs.

Alone again.

*The Yellow Note*

Everyone wanted to leave him. He was so worn out in his mind he couldn't even think. His attempt at trying to right the wrong had failed miserably. What to do now? He didn't even know if he had the gusto to try it again. What if it flopped again? Maybe stupid Chloe was right. Maybe none of this could be fixed.

When the dishwasher had been loaded, and everything cleaned up as much as possible, Pete turned off the lights on the first floor and headed upstairs. His feet did the walking without his brain, as he numbly made it to his bedroom, shutting the door and getting ready for bed. It was only eight, so early for him to be at this stage. But he was so tired. So done.

As Pete lay in bed, his eyes wandered around the dark room, first looking out a crack in the curtains to the moon that tried to peek in. Then he saw the yellow glow coming from his master bath to the right and finally his eyes rested on the nightstand where a small red light blinked on the cordless phone base. It was the line one button. Someone was on the phone.

Unable to stifle his curiosity, Pete took the phone in hand, pressed the mute button and put it to his ear.

"My fingers are still black." It was Heather, talking quietly.

"I know, mine too." Enter Chloe. "I even scrubbed with that lava soap."

"Okay, enough of that, I don't want to talk about it anymore. Since I don't have a car or a cell right

*The Yellow Note*

now, you're going to have to be my ride and my courtesy phone." Heather said. She giggled.

"And who do you call besides me?" Chloe laughed. "You have other friends?"

"Get over yourself." They both giggled a few moments and then there was a long silence.

"Do you ever think about God, Heather?" Chloe asked.

"What do you mean?"

"Do you ever wonder if it's not just a big game?"

"I've been there Chloe. I can't believe you're asking me about this. I thought we decided not to talk about Bible stuff. I have to bear it every Sunday and sometimes more. I'm just doing it so my parents don't get suspicious."

"Don't freak. I'm just asking."

"Are you saying you do?"

"On and off. Sometimes I hear my sister praying like a maniac in her bedroom and crying about me to God, and then she comes out and she's all peaceful and stuff."

Heather sighed. "Maybe she's faking it to make you want to follow God or something."

"Most of the time she doesn't even know I'm home." Chloe said. "I didn't think she'd turn to God after my parents died, but she did, and she's not depressed as she used to be."

"I'm kind of wigging out right now Chloe. You don't even sound like you."

"I'm just saying, what if God didn't take my parent from me. What if...what if it's all just a big lie that I believed."

*The Yellow Note*

"I don't know."

"I'm losing time."

Another long pause. "What?" Heather asked.

"I'm losing time. Spaces of my days that I can't remember. I just blank out then I come to and I can't remember what I was just doing."

"Look at how much trippin' we do. That's a given. I forget stuff too." Heather said.

"This isn't dope dumbness. I can tell the difference. It even happens when I'm not high. And it's getting worse. Ever since I started reading that book called "Spirit Guides", it's taken me over or something."

Heather was quiet.

"Are you still there?" Chloe asked.

"Yeah."

"Well?"

"I don't know what to say Chloe. I read parts of that book, and it's not happening to me."

"But I was really into it for awhile."

"Chloe, you're freaking me out."

"What if I've got demons or something."

"Are you high right now?" Heather asked.

"I smoked a little weed earlier."

"I think someone laced your bag or something. You should just sleep it off and drink lots of water."

"Heather, I'm serious. I'm not so high that I can't think."

"Fine. But I still don't know what to tell you and I'm getting tired."

"Me too I guess."

*The Yellow Note*

"I'll talk to you tomorrow. Don't forget to pick me up."

"I won't."

Pete pressed the off button on the phone and set it back on the charger. A bit of compassion rose up in him for Chloe. She'd always been so hard core, but this conversation she'd had with Heather wasn't anything like the character Pete was used to seeing in her. He shook his head and blinked. Was he actually thinking good thoughts about Chloe?

Pete rocked in his leather office chair at home as he stared out the window into the dark neighborhood. It was almost 9:00 p.m., early for him, but he just couldn't bring himself to do anything, but think.

Dinner hadn't been pleasant, again. No one would talk and of all people, Kristine was the first person to leave the table. She didn't seem angry, or irritated, just sad or something. Pete wasn't sure. He didn't really know if he should ask her.

Things were not good.

Pete was finding is hard to pray. He didn't really want to. It seemed boring, out of place. He was so out of practice that it just seemed useless. Nothing he tried to do to fix things seemed to be working. He'd probably screw the prayers up to.

His cell phone rang on his desk. Pete glanced at the number. It was the boss. Pete sighed and picked it up, hoping Frank didn't want him to come running down to the station right now.

"Hey Frank, what's going on?"

*The Yellow Note*

"I didn't interrupt dinner did I?"

"It's just after 9:00, who eats dinner at this time." Pete realized he was sounding a little short, but he wasn't going to apologize. He didn't feel like it.

"I do." Frank chuckled.

"Hmm."

"How's Kristine been?"

*Why are you asking?*

"She's fine."

"Lindsay has been meaning to have coffee with her, did she call?"

"I don't know, I don't think so." Maybe she had and that's why Frank was calling. Kristine was telling Frank's wife all about how terrible it was for her. Pete sighed.

"Oh. I'm sure she'll get around to it."

"What's the small talk all about Frank? You're usually a man of few words."

The pause was so long it made Pete feel uncomfortable. He sat up straighter in his chair, ready for whatever was about to come out of his boss's mouth.

"We found a match to the prints on the bottle." He said.

"Oh yeah?" Pete perked up. "Why didn't Brad call me?"

"Actually, the lab called for me to see the results. I was just finishing supper and, well, you know how it goes."

He was obviously stalling.

"And?"

*The Yellow Note*

"I went over them several times myself, double checking for errors, making sure files were labeled correctly. We can have her reprinted if you think there was a mistake, but we were very thorough in all the stages..."

"Her? Then it was Chloe." Pete couldn't help but smirk. To bad it was a sin to gamble cause he'd have won a bunch of money just now. He stood to pace his office floor.

"No."

Pete stopped. He frowned. "We didn't have any other girls on the list. The cheerleading squad all checked out okay."

"Yes we did."

"Who?"

"Your daughter."

"Heather?" Pete almost yelled. Now he was starting to get irritated. Frank was off his rocker and it was all some misunderstanding. It was probably a joke anyway. The boys had probably been planning it for awhile to get Pete to lighten up.

"Come on, who's were they?" Pete said.

"It was Heather's prints on the bottle." Frank said it firmly, clearly. Pete understood his words, but it just didn't make sense to him.

"You're joking, Brad put you up to this."

"No joke Pete."

Pete sat back down in his chair and closed his eyes. "The lab is wrong. I hope you know that. My daughter wasn't anywhere near that house that night."

*The Yellow Note*

"Like I said, you're welcome to have her come in a get reprinted but we're going to have an arrest warrant by tomorrow morning."

"What!" Pete slammed his desk with the palm of his hand. His face started getting hot.

"Prints on a murder weapon are more than enough to get an arrest warrant. You know that. Now, if you want to just bring her down here and not make trouble then—"

"Heather didn't have anything to do with this murder!" Pete looked up and saw Steve at the bottom of the stairs listening.

"I'm taking you off the case too. You're too close to it all now. I really should have done this sooner, when Heather's name first came up. I'd like you to take some vacation. You've got about two months of vacation and sick time that's accumulated over the past five years. I think now would be a good time to take it."

"It turns over every year. And you can't take me off the case, now more than ever."

"It's already done. I'll be helping from here on out. And if you create problems for us, I'll have you arrested too."

"Problems?" Pete scowled. "When have I ever caused problems for the team. I'm a good investigator, you need me there Frank!"

"Not like this you aren't. You won't be able to think rationally."

"I can't believe you're doing this to me." Pete took deep breaths and tried to calm himself but it wasn't working. He wanted to throw something

*The Yellow Note*

across the room, and he would have too had Steve not been watching him.

"I'm not doing anything but what's right. It has to be this way, like it or not."

"I'll be down there in a few minutes with Heather, so you can print her again."

"That's fine. We'll be waiting."

Pete shut his phone and slammed his desk one more time. Steve jumped. Pete had forgotten he was there.

"What's going on with Heather?" Steve asked. Pete shook his head and sighed, rubbing his face hard.

"I don't know Steve. I think they got her finger-prints mixed up with another set at the lab. It's making her look like she was in the house when that girl was murdered. But they're wrong. So don't worry about it."

Steve nodded and went upstairs.

If at anytime Pete didn't want to act like a Christian it was right now. His flesh wanted to run to the station and scream and yell and make a scene, demanding to know what the heck was going on. He couldn't do that. He didn't want to be locked up too.

Pete decided he'd talk with Heather, get her side of things. Not in an accusing way of course, if he knew how to do that. She was so touchy. Hopefully, she wouldn't freak out, but that was doubtful. He'd probably end up having to take her by the arm and drag her to the car. Maybe she'd even jump out of the car. He'd have to hand cuff her to the door or something.

*The Yellow Note*

He walked up the long flight of steps slowly, thinking, rolling over what he was going to say until he came to her door.

He knocked.

There was no answer.

"Heather?" He knocked again. Still, no answer. Dare he open the door? Pete turned it slowly. "Heather, I'm coming in okay." He pushed it open and saw the light was off.

"Heather," He whispered. "Are you sleeping?" There was no movement on the bed. He flipped the overhead light on and braced himself for the loud screech he'd get if she was trying to sleep.

She wasn't in the unmade bed.

He looked around her disastrous room and saw no one. Pete made his way across the room, trying not to step on anything, which was almost impossible. Someone should come up with a shovel and clear a path. The closet was empty except for clothes and plastic bins. Then over at her private bathroom, it was empty too.

Pete pursed his lips.

She was grounded, so she shouldn't be out doing anything. Not that grounding kept her at home. But now that Pete was home, she'd be more afraid to leave. Maybe.

He pulled his cell phone out and dialed Heather's number. It rang and rang and as Pete waited, he heard something down the hall. A familiar ring tone...a heavy metal song...from Heather's phone...in Pete's bedroom, hidden in one of his dresser drawers.

*The Yellow Note*

Pete closed his phone and rolled his eyes. He went to his bedroom and opened the drawer, pushed socks to the side and there it was, glowing with 'missed call' on the front. When he opened the phone it displayed his cell number. He slapped it shut and put it in his pocket next to his own.

Pete ran down the stairs, frantically searching the house, even turning over pillows on the sofa, looking under furniture. This wasn't good, not good at all. When he made his way downstairs he nearly collided with Kristine who had an arm load of neatly folded towels. He stumbled as he avoided her and landed himself right into the wall at the bottom of the steps. His elbow hit first, sending shock waves of pain up his arm and into his back.

"What are you doing?" Kristine stopped where she was, face concerned at first. When she realized Pete wasn't hurt too bad, her demeanor turned sour and she put a hand on her hip. "Why are you running around like a mad man. Good thing I haven't gone to sleep early in years."

"Have you seen Heather?" He rubbed his elbow, trying to ignore the numbness that was creeping down his arm into his hand.

"No."

"When did you see her last?"

"What is this, interrogation time?" Kristine huffed. She turned away from him and started for the downstairs bathroom.

"I can't find her."

"She's probably sleeping." She began putting the towels away in the cabinet next to the bathtub.

*The Yellow Note*

"She's not sleeping. I can't find her anywhere."

"Well, then she probably snuck out Pete." Kristine sighed and brushed past him into the hall. He followed her to the guest bedroom that she'd been staying in. Her work was spread out in an orderly fashion at the corner desk, everything was tidy. Pete had the urge to shove her papers off the desk and make things messy. Maybe that's what Heather felt when she did things like that.

"You say it so carelessly, like she's someone else's daughter."

"She acts like it." Kristine sat down on the bed and grabbed the remote and turned the TV on. She never watched TV. She just wanted to pretend she was busy. How dumb.

"Excuse me for interrupting you, but our daughter's finger prints were just found on the murder weapon used in the Thayer case. I need to find her and bring her to the station so that I can have her reprinted and prove to them that it wasn't her."

Kristine's mouth dropped open and she popped up out of bed like a Jack-in-the-box. "What?"

"You heard what I said. When's the last time you saw Heather?"

"I ah, I didn't. I haven't seen her since dinner...I guess." Kristine looked down at the floor and then around the room, her eyes wandering. Her lips twitched. "I haven't seen her since dinner."

"Where does she go when she sneaks out?" Before Kristine could answer, he knew. "Never mind. I know where she is." He turned on his heel

*The Yellow Note*

and rushed upstairs, got his keys and headed for the door.

"Where are you going?" Kristine ran after him out the front door.

"Chloe's Bennett's house."


Pete pushed the gas peddle almost to the floor as he raced down the freeway. He should have put the light up on top of his car, then he could have avoided the slow pokes.

He reached the other side of the city in no time and found the Bennett's place without much thought. He parked in their driveway and left the car running as he dashed up the sidewalk to the door and rung the bell over and over, until finally Chloe's sister opened the door.

"Detective Monson? What are you doing here?" Mara spoke through the screen to him, a concerned look to her face.

"Is my daughter over here?" He said.

"No, I don't think so." Mara turned to look at Chloe who was behind her, looking curiously at the door. "Chloe, is Heather here?"

"No. I haven't seen her since school." Chloe mumbled. Pete felt the frustration inside him building.

"I bet you know where she is!" He yelled through the screen. Mara jumped. Chloe's eyes got wide. "Tell me where Heather is! I know you know!" He reached for the screen door handle, but Mara was quick and locked it before he could get in.

*The Yellow Note*

"I don't know where she is." Chloe crossed her arms and walked closer.

"Yes, you do you little liar!"

"Hey!" Mara yelled. "Don't come around her and call my sister a liar. Your daughter is every bit as looney as her. Don't blame Chloe."

Chloe looked at her sister sideways. "I'm not looney."

"Chloe, if you don't tell me where Heather is I'll—"

"You'll what?" Chloe ran up to the door, pushed Mara out of the way and pressed her face up against the screen. "What will you do? Throw me in jail! HA! You've got nothing on me, and then I'd sue you for false arrest."

Pete took a step back, fuming. He squeezed his hands together, forcing the rage to remain under his control. If he didn't get some answers soon, who knew if he could hold it in.

"Just tell me!" He shouted. He could feel the veins in his face bulging, his neck muscles tensing. Both Mara and Chloe looked out at him like he'd gone insane.

"I'm calling the cops." Mara left them and ran for the phone.

"I don't know where she is. Can't you hear me?" Chloe said. "You'd better run, before your own friends stick you in a cell." The door shut with a loud wham, the glass in the screen door rattling.

Pete was alone on the front step in the dark. He turned from the house. The neighbors from across the street were watching through their window, and next door they were peering out from around the corner of their deck.

"What!" He screamed. "I'm a cop." And he hurried to his car and high tailed it out of the neighborhood.

Don had to fight the fear hard this time. He stood in the middle of his living room floor, new yellow note in hand, feeling his heart slamming against the inside of his rib cage. He was breathing deeply, the praying, breathing, then praying…it wasn't working.

The piece of yellow paper shook in his hand. Brownie stood next to him, whining, nudging his leg with her nose, leaving wet marks on his pants. He read the words again

*TO ANSWER YOUR QUESTION:*
*YOU SEE ME QUITE OFTEN.*
*AND YES, IT WAS ME WHO PUT THE*
*NOTE ON THE THAYER'S TREE.*
*I DON'T WANT TO HEAR*
*THAT NAME AGAIN.*
*IT MEANS HYPOCRITE TO ME.*
*I'M SO SICK OF*
*HYPOCRITES. EVERYWHERE I GO, THERE*
*THEY ARE. PITIFUL IDIOTS WHO ACT*
*HOLY BUT ARE TRULY THE MOST*
*UNRIGHTEOUS*
*THINGS ON THE PLANET! PLEASE, PLEASE,*
*I BEG YOU, DON'T TURN OUT*
*TO BE ONE OF THEM.*

*The Yellow Note*

It didn't sound like a blatant threat, but why was the writer so concerned that Don wasn't a hypocrite? What would happen if he were deemed hypocritical by the note writer?

Don wished he hadn't heard the noise tonight. He'd been reading Psalms, completely lost in the poetic words, when his thoughts had been interrupted by Brownie's small yip. He'd seen the hairs go up on her back and knew the writer had come again.

Don took calculated steps towards the telephone and put his hand on the receiver. He desperately wanted to call the police, at least it would ease his mind knowing that an officer would be circling the neighborhood.

But then why should he worry? The creator of the universe was on his side, the myriads of angelic hosts at his beck and call. Still, the natural world had such a grasp on his mind.

"Lord help me." He closed his eyes. "Why am I doing this? All logic wants me to call the police and be done with this nonsense." He listened, waited. Brownie finally left his side and lay down in her bed.

"How long am I supposed to do this?" Don sat down on the sofa. In just that instant, he knew it wouldn't be much longer, but he knew he had to wait it out. Still, it didn't make the waiting any easier.

# CHAPTER TWELVE

Once out of the Bennett's part of the city, Pete drove aimlessly, his mind full of thoughts, spinning, swirling thoughts about Heather.
*What if she did it?*
*Where is she?*
*She looks so guilty having run off.*
Finally, Pete realized he was just wasting time looking for Heather. There was no way he'd find her by himself, so he headed home. As Pete drove down his street, he noticed a squad car in someone's driveway. His driveway. There wasn't an ambulance. Lights weren't flashing. Why were they here?

Pete jogged up to the house and flung the door open when he got there. In the entry stood Frank, Kristine, Steve and an officer that was new on the job. At Pete's sudden entrance, the officer nearly un-holstered his gun. The scrawny kid tried to stare Pete down, but Pete stared back and the kid finally looked away.

"What are you doing here?" Pete said to Frank. The man turned to him with a stern face, arms crossed.

*The Yellow Note*

He looked like he was about to swear like he always did when he was mad.

"Actually, I was wondering what you were doing at the Bennett's house." He said. "Mara gave the station a call and said there was a belligerent cop demanding to have answers to where his daughter is."

"She knows where Heather is." Pete said. He took a few steps closer to Frank. "That little brat knows where Heather is. I'm sure of it. She's probably hiding her somewhere. She probably set this whole thing up so Heather would take the blame."

"Pete, you're out of control." Frank took a step towards him too.

"No, I'm not."

"You're not listening to reason. Heather ran because she's guilty. She ran because she knows she's been found out."

"That's not true!" Pete yelled. He made fists with his hands, squeezing them tight. As tight as he could. He might punch Frank. For just a moment Pete looked over at Kristine, her face was red from crying. Steve looked scared, but he seemed to be holding up.

"Why don't you listen to what your kid has to say, then you tell me." Frank nodded towards Steve. Steve looked at Frank, then at Pete and back to Frank.

"Go ahead, tell him Steven." Kristine said quietly.

"Heather snuck out that night dad. The night that girl was killed." He paused and looked back at Kristine. "I should have told you then, but I didn't want to, cause Heather always thinks I'm a little tattle tail. About a half hour after you guys left for

*The Yellow Note*

that church party, she left the house. She didn't say anything to me when I asked where she was going. She just walked out the front door. She didn't come home till midnight or something. Mom was in bed, you must have still been working. I heard something in Heather's room and I knew she wasn't home, so I went in there and she was crawling in through the window. She snapped at me and told me to get out of her room and not to dare tell on her."

Pete hung his head and closed his eyes.

*No. No, no, no! Steve's lying...*

Kristine turned away and started crying again. Frank's eyes were boring into Pete's when he looked up.

"What do you want me to say!" Pete yelled. He was shaking from head to toe, hot all over and he knew his face was beet red. "If you can find her arrest her. I don't even know where she is. Maybe you should check Chloe's house, get a search warrant and find my daughter!"

"We did. Her sister was kind enough to let some officers do a very thorough search of their house. Chloe was there at the time and she was as helpful as she could be, she was pretty worried about her friend as well."

"Yeah right."

Frank took two more steps towards Pete and pointed that fat finger in his face. His eyes narrowed. "You're about an inch away from having your gun and badge taken away. Don't push me."

Pete breathed heavy, squeezing those fists in and out. They were all watching him, waiting to see what

*The Yellow Note*

he would do. The young officer had a ready stance, his hand on his gun.

"Fine. Leave my house." Pete yanked his arm up and pointed at the front door. "Now."

Frank nodded once at Pete. "Be seeing you Kristine, Steve." He and the officer walked to the door. Frank turned one last time and looked at Pete. "Don't think we won't be watching."

Don shoved his students papers into a haphazard pile on his desk Thursday afternoon. It was almost 4:00 and he was done checking the assignment from yesterday, which was to write a synopsis of an hour long television show of their choice. Don realized now that he should have narrowed the choices down to suitable channels.

Half of the class summarized on decent shows, but the rest selected programs from the local and wild music channels, Gossip Hour and shows that were down right raunchy. With all that said, their grades weren't too poor this time around. Perhaps some of them were catching on.

Don had to mark down the three students who picked a nasty show, but made sure to write a note to the one student that his work was done well, but the topic was inappropriate.

And of course, as usual, there were a few missing papers. Among the missing, Chloe's and Heather's. Chloe had been in class the last two days, but Heather had been missing.

*The Yellow Note*

And there Chloe stood, in the doorway of his classroom, papers in her hand and a bag over her shoulder. She wore that sad, lonely face she'd been wearing the last few days.

"Mr. Graham?" She said.

"Hi, Chloe. What can I do for you?" He sat up and smiled at her.

"I forgot to bring my assignment from yesterday. I ran home to get it." She said. Don raised his eyebrows. What? She was actually doing some work?

"Oh, okay. That's good."

"Here." She walked into the room and handed him the assignment. At the top was typed, Synopsis of, 'Spirits In Darkness', history channel. By Chloe Bennett.

"Wow, Chloe. You typed this. You know this is supposed to be just the first draft, it didn't need to be typed." He said.

She nodded. "I know. My hand writing kind of sucks, I'm sure you know that. And I have a lap top so…"

"Well, good." He smiled again. "Say, have you seen Heather? The office never notified me if she was sick or something."

"Ah, I don't know when she'll be back." Chloe said. Her tone was off and she avoided his eyes.

"Is she alright?"

Chloe paused, shifted her weight and then sighed. "I'm sure it'll be all over the paper anyway. She ran away."

Whoa. That was unexpected. But why would it be in the paper?

"Really?"

"They think she murdered Laura." She looked at the ground. Don didn't know what to say. "Mr. Graham, do you believe in demons?"

"Yes, I believe demons exist." Why was she so talkative today? He almost felt weird about it. Could it be that she was trying to get him in trouble by getting him to talk to her about religious things. "Why do you want to know?"

Chloe still wouldn't look up at him. She began picking at the edge of her black, painted nails that were already chipped. "I was just curious after something I watched on the history channel. I used if for my assignment."

"Oh, I see." Don nodded. There was more to the story than this.

"So, can people have demons like they say?"

"In certain cases they can, especially if one were to purposely invite an evil spirit to live in them."

"If a person has a demon, can they get rid of it?"

"Of course. If a demonized person knows they need help and wants it, they can find someone who trusts in Jesus and knows their authority that Jesus gave them."

"What if a person was on a deserted island and there was no one like that around?" She said. Chloe fidgeted and kept her eyes focused on her hands.

"I guess that person would just have to call on the name of Jesus and believe in Him to help them." Don answered. He knew she was talking about herself now. Except, he wasn't sure why she was using the deserted island business.

*The Yellow Note*

"Would he?"

"Without a doubt. This show made you think didn't it?"

"Yeah." She took a few steps away from him. "I have to go now." And she left him in alone in the classroom.


It had been three days now. No sign of Heather anywhere. Dinner hadn't been made since and no one at the Monson house was talking. Not even Steve. The kid had been spending more time with his friend Zack, away from the house and if he was home, he shut himself in his bedroom.

Pete was restless. There was nothing to do. He'd driven past the Thayer's house at least ten times, taken drives out to the beach just to look at the water and contemplate life. This was not good. Now he was at home, in his office, staring at nothing.

Heather was out there somewhere, maybe half way across the country. And now she was on the wanted list. Pete had even seen her school picture on the news, along with her description. No one from the station had called him to see how he was doing. Maybe they were all told not to speak with him.

What a lousy week.

Deep inside Pete knew God wasn't punishing him, but he was beginning to wonder. Life had thrown him upside down and as much as he wanted to change it, he really didn't know what to do.

The house phone rang.

# The Yellow Note

Pete jumped. He looked at caller ID. and saw that is was Kristine's cell phone. Maybe she had some mean words to share with him. Reluctantly, Pete picked it up. "Hello?"

"Pete, Heather's in the hospital." She sobbed. Her cell phone was crackling. Pete sat up in his office chair and tried harder to listen.

"What?"

"Glenview Memorial Hospital. I'm almost there now." She sniffed and Pete heard a honk. Kristine shouted something at the driver who beeped her.

"What happened?" Pete hopped out of his chair and ran for the front door.

"I don't know. Get Steve, he'll be getting off the bus any minute now. I'm there now, so I'm going to let you go." She said.

"Okay." Click.

Pete found his keys and fumbled to unlock the garage door. He finally got out to his car and raced out of the driveway in time to see the school bus pulling up away from the stop at the end of the block. Steve was walking with his head down, back pack slung over his shoulder.

Pete slammed the brakes on next to him and pushed the passenger side door open. Steve looked confused.

"Get in." Pete said. Steve did as he was told.

"What are you doing?" Steve asked.

"Heather is in the hospital."

"Why? Is she okay?"

"I don't know, mom called me."

*The Yellow Note*

It was like a rabbit hunt inside the emergency room. No one at the counter knew anything about anything, until a nurse overheard Pete and directed him to a large waiting room on the other side of the hospital.

At last he found Kristine in the over populated room. And Chloe Bennett. She was talking to Kristine. When Pete saw her, his anger flared and he rushed over to them. Steve followed close behind.

"What is *she* doing here?" He demanded. Chloe turned around. Her eyes were red from crying.

"I brought Heather in, I—" Chloe tried to explain. Pete interrupted her.

"You were hiding her this whole time weren't you, little sneak." He got up right next to her and pointed in her face. Pete didn't care that the people closest to them were all listening.

"Heather came to my house, she—"

"I don't want to hear your story Chloe. Ever since Heather has known you she's gone down hill. I don't want you any where near her ever again."

Chloe's face got red and her eyes narrowed. Pete took a quick glance around. Kristine was holding on to Steve, They both looked shocked.

"You listen here, Mr. Monson." Chloe edged towards him, her finger now pointed in his face. Even though she was a foot shorter than him, her presence made him feel small. "Heather does what she does all on her own, I don't make her do crap. I didn't have anything to do with her running away, or her drug induced escapade today. She came to me. And if it wasn't for your sorry excuse of a Christian example, maybe your daughter would be more well behaved. Take a good look in that spiritual mirror of yours. You're pathetic."

And she pushed him and stormed out of the waiting area, leaving the entire crowd of people silent and starring at Pete like he was the one to blame. Some of them looked pretty disgusted. No doubt Jesus haters like Chloe.

"I can't believe you Peter." Kristine had rivers of black mascara running down her cheeks, even Steve looked like he was ready to cry.

And suddenly Pete felt his heart hit bottom.

Everyone hated him. Maybe God hated him too. He didn't even want to think about it right now, he just wanted to see Heather. "Where is she?" He said.

"They wouldn't let us in." Kristine answered.

"The doctors wouldn't tell you anything?" Pete looked down the hall where all the white coats were hurrying about tending to the large number of patients they had to see. His madness was mounting again. Didn't anyone know how to do anything around here.

"That's just ridiculous. Where are they?" Pete stomped down the hallway, passing room after room, ignoring common courtesy and ripping back curtains, so he could find his little girl. Patients gasped and doctors yelled at him, but he had to find Heather.

Finally, at the end of all the rooms, Pete stopped. She wasn't down here. Pete growled out loud. Kristine and Steve were standing at the opposite end of the hall from him, a doctor now standing next to them. Pete stomped back down towards the three-

*The Yellow Note*

some, sighing all the way. He was going to get some answers out of this doctor, and right now.

"Mr. Monson," The doctor stuck out his hand when **Pete** got to them. Pete didn't take it. Kristine cocked her head and gave him a dirty look.

"Where is she?" Pete said. The doctor took a second to answer.

"She's in the intensive care unit."

"Then take us to her."

"Pete, don't you want him to explain to us what happened?" Kristine said. A familiar look of irritation was on her face.

"I just want to see Heather, he can explain on the way."

"Follow me." The doctor said. "Her friend was very helpful to us in knowing the kind of drugs she was taking."

*Chloe, helpful?*

"Drugs?" Pete hurried along side the doctor, Kristine and Steve right behind them. "What was it?"

"A form of crystal meth. The friend was able to talk to your daughter a little before she fell unconscious and found that she had also been doing cocaine earlier in the day."

"She's unconscious?"

The doctor didn't answer. His face said it all. It wasn't good. "Yes. Because the drugs were both inhaled, they went to her blood stream rapidly. Her body was fully saturated with both substances when she was brought in. Mr. Monson, I have to be honest with you, she may not make it through the night." Pete stopped before they reached the elevator.

*The Yellow Note*

They all stopped.

Kristine had her hand over her mouth, tears welling up again. Steve just looked mad.

"Why, it's just drugs...can't you do something?" Pete said.

"She hadn't been breathing for at least a half hour before we were able to get her resuscitated, it's been touch and go since then." The doctor didn't have much of a bedside manner to him. Not that Pete cared, he was used to hearing the cold, hard facts, but Kristine and Steve weren't.

"She's not going to die!" Steve yelled. "Don't you people know anything! Jesus will heal her, she'll be okay!" Then he turned and took off down the hall from where they'd all come.

"Steve," Kristine called after him. "I'll get him." She hurried off down the hall after him.

"What does that mean?" Pete turned back to the doctor.

"She can't breathe or function on her own. There is little if any brain activity."

# CHAPTER THIRTEEN

Something was wrong.

Don could feel it in his spirit as he lay vegging out in front of the television. He'd been here since after dinner, laying on his back on the sofa, flipping channels, watching a little bit of everything.

At first he'd thought that feeling was because he felt useless in front of the tube, but it wouldn't go away. Nagging at the inside of him, prodding him. Finally, Don sat up and looked over at Brownie. She was sleeping, her head hanging off the side of her doggie bed.

He couldn't think of anything to pray about, so he just sat there, waiting, listening, speaking to God in his prayer language. On and on he went, his eyes closed, tongue moving as he spoke words he didn't even know existed.

There was hard, violent knocking at his door.

Don jerked. Brownie barked. Don got up and peered out the peep hole. In the orange glow of his outside light stood Chloe Bennett. Her strawberry blond hair a complete mess, make-up smeared

*The Yellow Note*

down her cheeks and eyes red as a lobster. She had something in her hand. He couldn't tell what it was. He didn't know if he wanted to open the door, but he did.

Chloe looked at him through the screen door.

"Hi Chloe, what brings you here?" Don glanced at his watch. It was after ten p.m. After ten? He'd been lounging around for nearly four hours! He should be in bed by now.

"Is this true?" She held up a little black Bible, shaking it next to the screen. How familiar that Bible looked...

"What?"

"Is this true? This Bible?" She flipped through the pages lined in gold. "Are the words in here true, can you live by them?" Her voice shook, her body too. She was livid, almost crazy.

"Yes..."

"I need to talk with you about it then." She said forcing her way into his house without being invited in.

"Um," Don looked behind him at Brownie, who stood in the middle of the living room, hair up on her back. "Okay." He held the door open, praying this didn't end in some kind of nightmare.

Chloe was shivering like it was cold. It was at least 75 degrees still, and humid. She looked down at Brownie who was sniffing her out, hair still up on her back. "Is the dog gonna bite me?" Chloe asked. She held her arms bent, away from Brownie.

"No." Don shut the door. "Go, lay down girl." He pointed at her corner. She looked up at Chloe,

*The Yellow Note*

back and Don and went to her bed. But she didn't lay down. She kept her eyes fixed on Chloe.

"Are you okay?" Don asked. He motioned towards the sofa but she didn't sit. Her whole body was tense.

Chloe stepped towards him and shook the Bible in his face. Her eyes were like a crazed animal out for the hunt. It made him nervous and he was already on the verge of sweating.

"IS – THIS – TRUE?!" She shouted. Her chest heaved in and out with breath. Chloe had her other hand clenched into a fist as it hung tight at her side.

"Yes, it's true." Don said. He watched her closely like Brownie, waiting for her next move.

"Heather tried to kill herself today." She said. *From one subject to the next...*Don frowned. He couldn't speak. If he could, he wouldn't have known what to say. He glanced at the phone. If he had to call the cops, he'd have to get around her first.

"She's been gone you know, and then she came to my house all tweaked out on drugs. She told me that she wanted to die, but she didn't say goodbye to anyone and she didn't really want to die after all." She paused for a minute, searching Don's face, maybe for some kind of answer. He was still trying to process this scene.

"Heather is brain-dead. That's what her mom said, I called her a little while ago." Chloe flipped open the small black Bible to the New Testament. "I need to know if this is right, if we can raise people from the dead, and heal the sick, all that stuff." She

219

*The Yellow Note*

pointed down at the words on the page, her finger jamming hard into the book. Don looked.

"Hello? Are you listening to me?" She poked the page over and over, until Don pulled himself from shock.

"Yeah, but…" He didn't know how to tell her, that only people who believed in Jesus could use His name like that.

"But what!?" She shouted all the sudden. Don jumped. Chloe's eyes got even more wild, furious looking. "Everyone always has a but! I'm so tired of being told I can't do something! Why do you think I came to your classroom and asked you about demons, huh?"

Don shook his head. He was getting more uncomfortable.

"Why do you think I stole your Bible?"

Don waited. He had no idea.

"Because I wanted someone to show me it was real. That all the stuff Jesus did was real. Laura didn't show me. None of the other Christian kids did. Heather's parents didn't. They're all lousy hypocrites!" She screamed so loud Don thought his ears would pop. Brownie was growling, body tense and ready to pounce if need be. Don had never seen his dog like that before. Maybe Chloe would manifest demons right here in front of him, in his own house. What a way to put his faith to the test.

"Okay…" Don said. He swallowed hard. His throat was very dry.

"But you," She pointed that slender finger in his face. "You were different right from the start, so I

# The Yellow Note

watched you. I've been watching your every move. At the grocery store, at school, when you got home from work. I followed you, like I followed Laura."

The adrenaline coursing through Don's body was making him weak in the knees and tingling all over. He was praying in the back of his head, unsure what to do at this point.

"I haven't seen you heal anyone, or raise anyone from the dead, but you treat people with respect, I've never heard you say a bad word about anyone, you're always smiling and there's something different about you." She said. "But why haven't you healed someone? Why haven't I heard of any of the miracles that Jesus did in the same sentence as your name?"

Don didn't know if this was a rhetorical question, or if he should answer. Before he could make a decision, Chloe yelled.

"Why?!"

"I guess because I haven't had the opportunity—"

"That's bull!" Chloe stomped her foot on the ground. Brownie stepped off her doggie bed. "That's a load of crap and you know it! There are at least three kids at school who have broken arms or legs, people have colds all the time, and I'm sure you know someone who's died. So tell me why."

Don hung his head and sighed. He might as well just let it all out, be honest with her and with himself. "Because I'm afraid."

"Why?"

"If it doesn't work, then I'll look like a fool." Tears came to his eyes as he realized what he was saying. All this time he'd been tricking his mind into

*The Yellow Note*

believing that he just *couldn't* do anything, because of the rules at school, or the situation, or the timing… but really, it was all because of fear.

"But you said this was all true." Chloe tapped the Bible with her hand.

"It is. It's my fault for not trusting the Word of God. I'm guilty."

Chloe's lip quivered and her face changed, softening. She took a few steps backwards and let herself fall to his sofa. "Finally, someone who admits it. Someone who doesn't twist the Bible to make it into what they want."

"I'm sorry." Now tears were coming down his cheeks, dripping off his chin and onto his chest. "Sorry that Christians haven't given a good example of what Jesus is like."

Chloe nodded. "I had demons you know." She said, looking at him for reaction. He wasn't surprised. "That's why I was asking you about them. But I did what you said and called out to Jesus and he took them away. I can think clearly now and I haven't forgotten a single piece of my day since then. I can even sleep better." She looked up at him suddenly, aware that he was crying.

"Did I scare you?" She asked.

Don sighed and laughed nervously. "A little, I'm still not sure what to think here."

"I stole this from your desk." She nodded her head down at his little Bible in her lap. "I didn't want to tell my sister that I was asking questions. She'd have probably said, 'I told you so'."

*The Yellow Note*

"I told you so? Are you saying that you accepted Jesus?"

A big smile crept up on Chloe's face. Her eyes lit up and Don could see what he hadn't seen before. She hadn't been raging in an evil way just a minute ago, but in a righteous way. She had wanted the truth.

"Yes." She said. A wave of relief flooded over Don and his legs got so week he stumbled back into the chair behind him.

For the past ten minutes his mind had been on a spiral downward and now he was being yanked back up like a roller coaster.

"Well, that's certainly not what I had expected when you showed up at my door." Don said. There was a long string of silence and Don started to feel uncomfortable, but Chloe didn't seem to be at all. He tried to lighten up a bit.

"So, you're going to pray for Heather?"

"Yes. And she's going to be healed. I just have to find a way to get to her room at the hospital. Her dad doesn't want me to see her ever again." Chloe pursed her lips. "I have to go now." She stood up and walked to the door. After she pulled it open, she turned around and held the Bible out to Don.

"Here." She said. "I'm sorry I took it."

"No, keep it." Don smiled.

"Really?"

"Really. I can get another one."

"Thanks." She looked down like it was the best thing she'd ever been given. Don knew that it was.

\*     \*     \*

*The Yellow Note*

Like most Sunday mornings, Kristine and Pete were at church again, mingling in the foyer and greeting their friends. Well, Kristine was mingling, Pete was standing at the far corner of the foyer with his hands in his pockets, as usual, looking board and trying not to be noticed by anyone.

*Why can't he just be more outgoing!* Kristine thought, as she put on her happy face. She closed her eyes briefly to shake off her irritation and when she opened them again, a peculiar thing had happened. Something had changed.

Everyone was smiling, but Kristine noticed that many of the people that walked around the large church were wearing clown outfits. *What?!* Just a minute ago the church folk were all wearing their Sunday best, now many of them were ready to go to the circus?

Kristine glanced Pete's way again and saw that he too was wearing a clown suit. She gaped at him and then scowled. *Some kind of joke this is!* No one else seemed to be aware of it, or at least they were pretending not to notice. They all looked so stupid!

Kristine stood in shock, knowing something was wrong. This wasn't something she'd missed. No one but her seemed to realize that people were wearing bright colored wigs, white facial make-up and huge red noses. The people still wearing regular clothing went about the church as usual, talking and laughing, making their rounds about the church.

Horrified and confused, Kristine ran to the woman's bathroom where she came face to face with the pastor's wife and another woman from the

## The Yellow Note

church who was crying. The pastor's wife, who was in regular clothing, tried to console the woman in clown get-up and gave her a tissue. Soon the woman dried her face and took a deep breath to calm herself. The pastor's wife gave her a quick hug and left the bathroom.

That same woman the pastor's wife was talking with, face red and eyes puffy, found a mirror and spoke to herself. "I can't go out there like this. They'll all know something happened..." Her voice trailed off as Kristine watched the woman pick up a heap of clothing from the floor. It was a clown suit. She pulled on the jumper arrayed with colorful zigzags, put a huge purple wig on her head and applied the happy face and bright eyed make-up. Satisfied with how she looked the woman brushed passed Kristine with the fake, painted smile and exited the bathroom.

Outside the door Kristine heard someone ask the woman if something was wrong, The woman simply replied that she'd gotten something in her eye.

Feeling bewildered by the situation, Kristine made her way to the mirror and starred at her own reflection. Her heavily painted face had an exaggerated smile and the clown outfit she wore resembled something she'd seen at the county fair once. Her wig was neon yellow, curly and long. The oversized ruffled dress had multi-colored polka dots and lace trim and her red shoes were at least five sized too big. Kristine looked hideous, but no one else seemed to care or notice, because they too were adorned in the same fashion.

*The Yellow Note*

Suddenly, the lights in the bathroom flashed off, leaving her in the complete darkness. In just a moment a single flood light shown down on her from above, so bright that she had to squint until her eyes adjusted.

In the mirror she still saw herself. Only herself. No bathroom or other women. She was all alone.

"How do you look?" Said a booming voice from wherever the light was coming from.

"Silly." Kristine said, shrugging her shoulders.

"Would you rather take it all off?"

"Yes."

As soon as she answered, a pounding water fall blasted at her from all angles, tearing the clown suit off and washing all the make-up away. When the water stopped, Kristine looked into the mirror again. She was clothed in one of her best work skirt suits, but it was tattered on the edges, ripped in several places and dirty. If she was wearing regular make-up, she couldn't tell. All the little imperfections she tried to hide every morning with foundation and power were all exaggerated in the blaring light. Her hair was dull and ratty, her eyes lifeless.

Kristine wasn't pleased with the awful way she looked and almost wished she could have that Bozo attire back.

"Every day you cover what reality is." Said the Voice. "Under your mask is who you want to hide. You can't hide from Me."

"But what happened? I don't really look like this, do I?" Kristine glanced down at her body.

"Not on the outside. You've become so involved with your work, so angry with your husband for doing the same, that you've become calloused to My voice. I've been trying to show you what the state of your own spirit is, but every time I do, you put on a false face. A mask. You've cared so much about your outward appearance and how your family is portrayed, that you've been blind to the truth."

The searing hot pain in her heart was terrible, but it felt good at the same time. Something was changing inside and though it hurt so bad, she wanted it to continue.

"You're family's life is on the line. Your husband is wrestling with his own fears and masks. Your daughter is on the fence, ridding between life and death and your son is struggling to seek Me and not give up."

"It's all my fault?" Kristine felt her lip quiver.

"No. But you and your husband have neglected to seek Me first. Because of this, things have progressed rapidly towards the evil one. I'm urging you to repent and pray. Things are coming that you are unaware of, things that can only be changed by prayer. I don't have many in this city who are willing to pray anymore." The Voice paused. "I need you." As he spoke, Kristine felt His heart pulling her, wanting her.

"What will happen if I don't pray?"

"The darkness to come is incomprehensible to your mind. And it will spread if things stay the same."

"What should I do?"

*The Yellow Note*

"Repent. Pray. Believe."

The Voice and the light receded leaving Kristine alone.

The faint sound of a steady beep and a whooshing sound knocked at the edge of Kristine's mind. She rolled her eyes around behind her eyelids and finally pulled them open. The room was dim, light from the hall the only thing illuminating Heather's hospital room. She was still in a coma. Still being kept alive by those machines. Kristine's heart ached, tears came to her eyes as she slid her chair closer to Heather's bed and grabbed her daughters hand.

"Heather," She said quietly. "I'm so sorry. I'm sorry I work so much, I'm sorry that I haven't been there to hold you when you need someone. I want things to be different. Things will be different." Kristine paused. "I'm sorry Jesus, forgive me, I need you to help me be strong and believe. I need you to help me change."

\*     \*     \*

Three weeks and two days.

That's how long Pete had been eating this lousy hospital cafeteria food. He went through the short line slowly, letting the women with hairnets put whatever items he chose on his plastic tray. It reminded him of school. Only this was not school. This was horrible. This was wrong. His daughter laying unconscious three floors up being kept alive only by machines.

*The Yellow Note*

The pastor had been here to pray.

The intercessory team had been here to pray. Pete had prayed, Kristine had prayed, Steve had prayed… the entire church was praying for them. For Heather. The past two Sundays had been hard. Everyone felt sorry for them. They all had long faces and words of condolence.

Pete wanted to scream at them and tell them it was all their fault she hadn't been healed yet. But that would be stupid. He was just as much at fault.

Pete walked over to a small two person table where Kristine already sat, picking at her food. He sat down in front of her on the other side of the table and watched her move a bowl full of macaroni and cheese around with her plastic fork. Her chin rested on her left hand. She was dressed in sweatpants and a loose t-shirt, hair up in a bun, no make-up. Very unlike her. She hadn't been to work much. Hadn't done much but sleep in that downstairs bedroom at home and sit by Heather's side all day long.

"How much longer are we going to do this?" Pete asked. Kristine looked up at him with her tired eyes.

"Do what? Eat here? I don't want to cook dinner for the three of us. I haven't bought groceries for two weeks, we don't even have anything I can make." She said.

"Not food, I mean coming here. Heather isn't even in there. It's just a body fed oxygen and food through tubes. That's not living. Nothing has changed. You heard the doctor, her body can't function on it's own, she'll be a blob the rest of her life."

# The Yellow Note

Kristine's eyes narrowed, her face turned red. "Are you suggesting that we just pull the plug?"

"She's not there Kris. We can't keep doing this." Pete looked down at his tray of untouched food. Maybe he'd get to it by the time it was cold. Or maybe not at all. He'd already lost a few pounds.

"We can keep doing this as long as it takes." She said defiantly, now eating faster.

"It could be years."

"Are you concerned about money?" She kept her eyes on the macaroni as she piled it on her fork, strings of cheese pulling away from the bowl.

"No, I'm not concerned about money." Pete sighed. "Insurance will take care of most of it, and we have enough anyway. What I don't want is to do this for the next 10 years, watching Heather in this state of nothingness as we all go on with our lives."

"So, you've given up then." She glared at him.

Had he? "No…"

"Yes, you have. You've given up on God and what he can do."

"God can do anything…I just don't know if I believe — "

"Shut up Peter!" Kristine stood up all of the sudden and grabbed the side of her tray. "Don't say those words out of your mouth! I believe and I don't care how long it takes, Heather will wake up and she'll be fine cause we prayed for her and we have Jesus. That's all we need."

She shoved her chair into the table so hard that it almost spilled Pete's milk. "Now, I'm going up to Heather's room. And I'm going to read her scriptures

*The Yellow Note*

about healing. Her body hears it and she's going to get up. If you can't come up believing, then don't come at all."

Kristine walked away, her face beet red and jaw set. Pete sighed again and looked down at his food. Yuk. But he had to eat something or his pants wouldn't fit in another week. He was already down to the last notch on his belt.

The black garbage bag made James Riley cringe. The menace in his brain. The secret of all secrets. The unholy, sick bag that haunted his dreams and made him nervous. Actually, it was the contents of the bag. He didn't want to look in there. But he'd probably have to see it again. Probably today.

He stared at it, high in his closet, stuffed into the corner of the top shelf, unnoticeable to anyone else, but the edge of it stuck out, easy for James to see. He'd seen it every day for the last month. He couldn't forget about it. He'd tried. He should have just thrown it away in some random alley garbage dumpster. But for some reason he'd kept it. For some reason it had to be hidden. For a certain time. For today.

It seemed like an eternity that he stood and looked at that garbage bag, its alarming contents still vivid in his head, until finally, James reached up and pulled it down, careful not to rip the black plastic or touch too much of the bag. He didn't want to disturb what was inside.

It was time.

Time to unveil the kept secret.

*The Yellow Note*

James looked at his digital clock. It was almost six p.m. Almost time for dinner. He couldn't wait. Even though he'd miss dinner and cause a chaotic night for his family, he had to do this now. It couldn't wait. Not one day more. Not even until after dinner.

His heart thumped hard as he held the bag in his hand by the knot he'd made when he'd put the contents inside. He could feel the sweat forming in beads on his face, his breathing quickened.

James left his bedroom and went upstairs. His mother was in the kitchen taking a pan of lasagna out of the oven. Garlic bread sat steaming on the stove top and a colorful salad was prepared in the large glass bowl she always used. It looked wonderful. Scrumptious. He wanted to eat, but the smell that was normally tantalizing made James gag. He might not be able to eat for hours and his stomach grumbled, but he just couldn't now.

"Hey James," His mother smiled as she saw him standing there. He couldn't answer her. She glanced down at the bag. "Garbage day was yesterday." She said.

James nodded. He wiped the sweat off his forehead with the back of his hand. She frowned at him and tilted her head to the side. "Are you okay?" She asked.

"Uh, I have to go do something." He told her, his heart slamming so hard against his chest it was making him feel light headed.

"I'm just about to put dinner on the table, can it wait?"

*The Yellow Note*

"No." He said firmly. James looked down at the bag. "I'm sorry I'm going to miss dinner, but I have to do this. You and dad go ahead. I'll give you a call if I'm not back in an hour."

His mom frowned. "What's going on?"

"I'll tell you later, I have to go now. I'm sorry." He turned away, careful not to let the bag hit his leg as he walked.

Pete didn't know if he truly believed. So he didn't go up to Heather's room before leaving the hospital. If Kristine was there she'd pounce on him about faith and wouldn't stop. Or else she'd ignore him and continue reading scripture to Heather. Either way his presence wouldn't be welcomed by his wife. So he left.

It was six when he left the hospital, it's starchy walls and bland food. There wasn't anything to eat at home, but the thought of take out came to mind. Maybe Chinese or something. Not pizza. They served that at the hospital.

And television. A good movie or something on National Geographic would take him away from the reality of his situation.

The first thing Pete did when he got inside the house was find the phone book. Steve came walking down the steps, somber, but with a half smile. At least he was trying to be in good spirits. It made Pete feel a little more at ease. Pete suddenly felt bad because the kid had been home since 2:45 and no one had bothered to think of him for dinner. Good thing Pete hadn't eaten yet.

"Hi buddy." Pete smiled at his son as he came and stood by him.

"Hi." Steve said. "How's Heather?"

"The same." Pete nodded. "Mom's with her. I was gonna order some Chinese, want some?"

"Sure." He shrugged. "Whatever you have. I'm not picky." Pete knew he wasn't. A very good quality about him. He had a lot of good qualities.

Pete ordered for them and sat down on the living room sofa. The t.v. wasn't on. He just stared at the screen wondering if he should grab the remote. Steve came and took the other side of the sofa.

"I'm sorry I missed your games Steve." Pete said. The boy shrugged and looked up at his dad.

"It's alright. There will be other games."

"No, it's not alright. I've been way too busy with my work. There's a million excuses I could give you, but none of them are really good reasons not to be a good father and husband. I don't even know where to start, or how things got this way."

Steve didn't say anything, just looked at Pete with thoughtful eyes.

Pete sighed.

His cell phone vibrated in his pocket. Pete pulled it out and saw that it was Frank. He rolled his eyes.

"Hello?" He answered, his tone obviously agitated.

"Pete, you know Zack Hartson?" Frank asked.

"Yeah, why?"

*The Yellow Note*

"We've got him down at the station right now. He says he has something to tell you. He won't tell us what it is except that it's very important."

"Does it have something to do with the case?" Pete sat up straighter and looked over at Steve. He'd have to leave the kid alone again.

"Zack won't say a peep without you being here."

"Does this mean I'm back on the case then?"

"Don't push it." Frank grunted. "I just need you to get down here and talk to him so we can figure out what the heck is going on around here. I've tried to reach his mother, but she's at work and she doesn't have a cell phone. Zack is unsure where his mother works at this time of day. Could be one of three places and we tried all of them."

"Fine. I'll be there in a little while." Pete shut the phone and stuck it back into his pocket. Steve's eyes looked a little sad now.

"Do you have to go somewhere?" Steve asked.

"Yes. But I'm going to wait until the food gets here, and I'm going to eat with you and then I'll leave."

Steve smiled. "Okay."

"Do you know why Zack would be down at the police station?"

Steve frowned and shook his head. "No."

"He told my boss that he has something important to tell me."

"Maybe he wants to tell you his mom beats him."

"Does she?"

"I don't know for sure. He never told me, but all those bruises and stuff. I told you about it before."

*The Yellow Note*

"But why would he go down to the police station to tell me. Why wouldn't he just come here?"

Steve shrugged.

The doorbell rang. The food. Pete got up and answered the door, paid the Asian man who held a large, white paper bag and said thanks as he left. It smelled wonderful.

# CHAPTER FOURTEEN

Kristine held Heather's limp hand as she sat next to her, reading scripture and praying. Every few lines she would look up at Heather's face, then at the beeping machine next to the bed, at the pump that breathed for her and the IV's that were feeding her.

About fifteen minutes ago, Chloe Bennett had called Kristine to ask if it would be alright if she came to visit Heather. Kristine said yes. Maybe to spite Pete in a way. He'd probably gone home anyway, after what she'd said to him. She did feel kind of bad. But then again, she didn't want any unbelief hanging around Heather. Their daughter would get up out of this bed and walk out of this room on her own two feet. Not in a body bag. And if Pete couldn't believe with her, then he could just stay away.

Chloe walked in the door shyly and looked around the room, maybe scanning for Pete. She closed the door behind her, eyes locking in on Heather and all the wires and tubes attached to her body.

"Hi Chloe." Kristine smiled at her. Chloe smiled back. It was the first time Kristine had ever noticed

*The Yellow Note*

her arch her mouth upward instead of towards the floor. Even though Chloe still wore black clothing and had her face plastered with dark makeup, Kristine could see something different in her eyes.

"Hi." Chloe said. She stood on the other side of the bed facing Kristine. "It's just you?"

"I think Pete went home. Don't worry about him, he's just scared."

"He doesn't like me very much."

"He doesn't know you, Chloe." Kristine said. "I don't either. I let you come because I know you and Heather were...are, best friends." Chloe nodded.

"Okay then...I guess I just do it." She said. She looked at Heather. Kristine frowned. Huh? Chloe put one hand on Heather's forehead and one hand on her chest.

"What are you doing?"

"What someone should have done weeks ago." Chloe said. She glanced at Kristine for just a moment, her eyes flashing with fire and...what was she going to do? Kristine stood fast, the Bible that had been in her lap fell to the floor.

"Chloe, what are you doing?"

She didn't answer. "Heather, I command you by the Spirit of God, to wake from this coma and become alive and awake." Chloe's voice was firm, loud, but not screaming and it sent chills up Kristine's spine. She took a step back. She didn't know what to say. Was Chloe a Christian? She sure hadn't been acting like one all this time her and Heather had been friends...

Something was in the room.

*The Yellow Note*

Kristine turned her head from side to side, using her eyes to move more than her body. It was thick, vibrating, and intense. She had goose bumps all over her skin.

The heart monitor suddenly stopped, one long beep replacing the steady rhythm that Kristine had grown accustomed to over the past weeks. Chloe stood back and smiled. *What on earth! Did she just kill my daughter?*

A second later the machine started up again, this time beating wildly and without pattern. And Heather moved. Kristine's mouth hung open. She stared down at Heather's face seeing her eyes rolling around behind her eyelids.

The next moment a nurse burst into the room, three other doctors right behind her. "What happened?" The one male doctor asked as he rushed to Heather's side, pushing Chloe away in the process. Kristine only looked at him. She didn't know what to say, she didn't know herself. Chloe stood in the corner watching, her eyes lit up and her face glowing with a smile.

The four medical staff rattled off a heap of jargon Kristine couldn't understand and suddenly one of them yelled, "She's trying to breathe!" Kristine leaned as close as she could to see between them, but couldn't tell what was happening. Gurgling noises and choking and a strange sound Kristine couldn't put a finger on. Then coughing.

"Sit her up!" The nurse yelled.

*The Yellow Note*

Kristine looked back over at Chloe. The girl was beside herself with joy, tears streaming down her face as she watched the action.

"What's happening?" Kristine asked. She moved to the end of the bed to get a better look. The tube that was once helping Heather breathe lay on the blanket next to her. Kristine's heart beat furiously within her.

*Is she really awake?*

Heather's face was red as she dry heaved and coughed. Her arms flailed about as the staff held her down. Within a few minutes everything settled down and Heather lay against the upraised bed, her hands calmly beside her, taking deep, careful breathes.

"Heather?" Kristine's lip trembled. She put a hand to her mouth to keep it still. "Heather, is me, mom."

"Mom?" Heather's voice was raspy and she coughed again. Her eyes rolled around behind her closed lids. The doctor took a small light and peeled back one of her lids to look at her pupil. Heather flinched, closed her eyes tight and pushed at his hand. "That's too bright." She said, again hoarse.

"Heather, my name is Doctor Caleb. I've been looking after you for the last twenty-three days." The doctor told her. The other three were checking the monitors and the brain wave chart that was slowly being fed through a machine to the left of Heather's bed. They looked like they were all in shock.

"Twenty-three days?" Heather said. She coughed again. "I'm so thirsty…" she said.

*The Yellow Note*

"Okay, we'll get you some water." Caleb motioned to one of the nurses to get the water and she left the room. "Can you open your eyes?"

Heather squinted, slowly opening one eye, then the other. She blinked several times like her eyes were dry. She looked past Kristine. "Chloe?"

"Heather, can you focus on me for just a minute?" The doctor held the little light again.

"Not if you're going to beam me with that thing again. I can see fine." Heather said. She struggled with her arms to push herself higher in the bed.

Kristine could hardly contain herself. She has so much to say to her, but nothing would could out. She just stood there, watching Heather's every move, tears coming out in rivers.

"What's the last thing you remember Heather?" The doctor asked her. Heather kept her eyes open but squinted.

Heather focused in on Kristine and her face got sad. She looked down at her thin arms. "I took some drugs and I think I found Chloe's house..." And then Heather burst out in sobs, her whole body shaking. Kristine couldn't help herself. She forced the doctor out of the way and got onto the bed with Heather, wrapping her daughter with her arms. Heather held on, as tight as her frail body could and they wept together.

"I was in hell!" Heather cried. "It was dark and people were screaming...I can't even describe it." She caught her breath and pulled back from Kristine. Chloe was at her side now, a box of tissue in her hand. Heather pulled a piece out. "Because I rejected

*The Yellow Note*

Jesus." She wailed even harder now, sending her into another coughing fit. "I went to hell because I rejected Jesus."

The doctor was wide eyed, staring down at this girl who'd just been brought back from a world of sleep. Everyone was quiet for a minute while Heather calmed herself.

"Sometimes people who are in a coma see very strange and seemingly real thing—" Caleb tried to speak, but Heather cut him off. She turned her head to face him.

"I was there. I know what I saw, I know where I was. I tried to kill myself...I did kill myself and I went to hell because I chose evil and not Jesus. And I would have been there forever except that...I'm not. I'm here." As if Heather suddenly realized that something had to have happened to get her back from the grave, she looked at Kristine. "Did you pray for me?" She asked.

"We all prayed for you." Kristine said. "But it Chloe that prayed for you just now."

Heather looked over at her friend who still had the tissue box ready. Her face was bright, smiling, but a streak of black tears on both of her cheeks.

"Chloe?" Heather looked confused.

"I follow Jesus now." Chloe said.

Kristine gaped at her. Well obviously, but she hadn't known it. Heather looked just as surprised.

"Heather, we're going to need to run some tests and—" Doctor Caleb was cut off again, by Heather.

*The Yellow Note*

"I don't want to do any tests right now. I want to talk to my mom and my friend..." Chloe looked at Kristine. "Where's dad and Steve?"

"They're at home, I'll call them." Kristine looked down at her cell phone in her shaking hand. So much had just happened...she hadn't even been aware of it as Heather was waking up, but a new sense of change had come into Kristine's heart. She wanted things to be good again. She wanted to sleep in the same bed as Pete, she wanted to sit next to him on the sofa and have conversations with him like they used to.

Kristine's lip trembled.

"Mom?" Heather asked. Kristine didn't look up. "Are you okay?"

"I'm fine." She nodded as tears spilled over her bottom eyelid onto her cheeks. "I'm just thinking. Things are changing..."

"My sister did it." Zack said quietly. He stood in front of Pete, staring down at the floor, picking at the calluses on his hands. Pete shook his head. Those were the first words the kid had said to him. When Pete had said hi upon seeing Zack in one of the interviewing rooms, he'd only nodded. Frank and Brad were both there too looking stressed and anxious.

"What did she do Zack?" Pete pulled one of the chairs out and had Zack sit down. Pete sat on the edge of the table and waited.

"She killed that Laura girl." He said. The three men in the room were all ears. Pete looked up at Frank and Brad who were standing against the wall.

*The Yellow Note*

"How do you know this?"

"I was there when she left and I was there when she came back. She had blood on her...I heard what Grace and James were talking about." Zack told him. He was still focused in on that callous that had nearly come off by now.

"How long have you known about this?"

"Since that day. I'm sorry I didn't tell you Mr. Monson." Zack finally looked up. "I was really scared. I thought she might hurt me like she does when she's mad."

"Grace hurts you?"

He nodded. "Please don't tell her I told you."

"I won't tell her." Pete shook his head. "How does she hurt you?"

"She hits me."

Alas, the reason for the bruises. Pete sighed, as much for frustration as for relief that he now knew it wasn't Zack's mother. "Can you remember what happened that night Zack?" Pete's cell phone vibrated in his pants pocket. He couldn't bother with that now, this was very important.

He nodded.

"Where's your mom at right now?"

"She's working, I'm not sure where right now. It's okay, I don't need her here. I can tell you."

"Legally you have a right to have your mom with you Zack, are you sure you don't want to wait until we can get her down here?" Pete looked over at Frank and twirled his finger in the air to ask if sound and video were recording. Frank nodded.

*The Yellow Note*

"Okay, my friend Brad and my boss Frank are going to leave now, I'm going to stay and sit here with you." Pete stood up and grabbed a chair for himself to sit in, get to Zack's level to make the boy feel more comfortable.

To Pete's surprise, Frank didn't object and he left the room with Brad. Not like they weren't going to be right behind that tinted glass anyway.

"Okay, go ahead and tell me as much as you remember, in order. I may ask you questions in between, but keep on going until I do okay?"

Zack nodded again. "Mom was at work that night. Grace decided to stay home with me and watch movies and have pizza. She's actually pretty fun to be around when she's not acting weird."

"What do you mean by weird?"

"She's supposed to be on medication, but she forgets to take it sometimes. When she doesn't take it she gets really sad or really angry all a sudden, some times she just freaks out and throws things and has a fit. She likes to hit me." He stared down at his hands.

Pete pursed his lips and crossed his arms.

Zack looked up at Pete and Pete nodded for him to continue.

"We were right in the middle of a movie and she got up and said she had to run an errand and made me promise not to tell mom or anyone she'd left at all. She told me that if anyone asked about it I was to tell them she was with me that whole night watching movies. When I asked her what she was going to do, she told me that it was a surprise for Laura. I knew she was planning a party for her so I didn't think

*The Yellow Note*

anything of it. I watched the rest of the movie by myself."

Zack took a long, deep breath. "She came home hours later."

"About what time? Do You remember?"

Zack shrugged. "I don't know, I wasn't really paying attention to time. It was dark, that's all I remember."

"Okay, go ahead and finish."

"She was bloody and sweaty and her face was all red...her eyes were like demons or something. She had this black ski mask in her hand. Grace just looked at me and then ran to her room. I had no idea what she'd done till I heard some people talking at school and the rumors about someone wearing all black and a ski mask.

And then Grace tried to get me to put her bloody clothes into a bag and burn them somewhere far from the house, but I wouldn't do it so, she had one of her fits and started punching me and throwing me around. I ran to a corner and hid until she stopped. She never said anything about it since. I never brought it up cause I thought maybe she'd kill me too."

Tears streamed down Zack's face, dripping onto his hands that were in his lap. "I wanted to tell you Mr. Monson, I just couldn't. She's my sister, I love her."

"I know Zack, I know." Pete smiled at him warmly. "You're telling us now, that's all that matters. Do you know if anyone was with Grace when she killed Laura?"

"I don't know."

*The Yellow Note*

"Did you ever see her writing on little pieces of yellow paper?"

"Not that I can remember."

Pete nodded. "I'm going to need you to stay here until we can get a hold of your mom okay."

"Sure." Zack wiped his face with the hem of his t-shirt.

"You just sit tight and I'll be back in a little while." Pete stood up and left Zack in the room by himself.

\*     \*     \*

Brownie yipped five seconds before the doorbell rang just after dinner. Don glanced over at the door, he wasn't expecting anyone. He'd just sat down to the nightly news with a bowl of popcorn. He intended on having a nice, peaceful evening.

Don got off the sofa when the bell rang a second time. When he peered through the peep hole he saw Chloe on his doorstep, dressed in her usual black attire and looking ragged. He'd almost expected to see her dressed in...well...normal clothing after giving her life to Jesus. But then again, Jesus didn't really care about what kind of clothing people wore.

Don opened the door and smiled.

"Hey Chloe." He said.

She didn't smile. From behind her back, she pulled out a pile of crumpled notes, her hands shaking as she showed him. Don wasn't sure what she wanted and looked closer at the papers.

Something familiar.

*The Yellow Note*

In fact, it looked like the same paper from the pad he had in the little end table. The same papers he'd used to write back to...

"What are these?" He asked, knowing, but not wanting to know. His heart thumped hard.

"I just couldn't keep quiet anymore." She said, unfolding one of the notes. "See, your writing." She showed him all of them, one at a time, making reality set in even hard for Don. "I did it, Mr. Graham."


Pete looked at Zack through the window in the door. The boy had his head down on his arms on the table now, resting but not sleeping. Frank had tried to reach Ms. Hartson again, but only got her voicemail, he'd left a message so now they played the waiting game.

Poor Zack.

Pete turned from the window and leaned against the hallway wall where he and Frank stood. They hadn't said much.

"Frank." A voice echoing from down the hall. Pete turned and saw Brad walking with James Riley right behind him. James had a black garbage bag in his hand, he held it away from his body, careful not to let it hit his legs as he went.

"James has something he'd like to share with us."

Frank nodded and motioned towards the room across from Zack. Because of the loud talking, Zack looked over through the window and when he saw James with that black bag his eyes grew wide.

*The Yellow Note*

There was a murderer on his front step. Don was standing with the screen door wide open, Chloe Bennett shaking wildly and starring into his eyes. Both of them were silent, unmoving.

Finally, Chloe spoke.

"Aren't you going to say anything?" She let her hand drop to her side, the notes still grasped tightly between her small fingers.

Don thought for a moment. "Chloe, I have to be honest, I'm not sure if I should call the cops or hear what you have to say first."

Her face fell sad. "I know I should have told them sooner…I probably should be at the cop shop right now instead of here, but I'm scared I'll get in trouble."

Don hesitated. Was she serious? Didn't she know the consequences of killing someone? "Um, I guess you'll just have to prepare yourself for whatever may come, but keeping it from the law is only going to make things worse."

Chloe blinked and stared at him strangely.

"You think I killed Laura?" She said.

Don nodded. He was too nervous to answer.

Chloe chuckled lightly. "Oh my gosh. I didn't kill her. I wrote that note on that tree outside her house, and I hated her, but I didn't murder Laura."

"What about the notes you gave to me, you made it sound like—"

"Like I hated her. I wouldn't have done something that stupid. I knew the cops would be right on my tail if anything like that went down."

249

*The Yellow Note*

Don sighed heavily, letting out his tension with his breath. "You really had me going there for a minute."

"Sorry."

"How come you didn't tell me about the notes? You saw me every day at school, I would have gladly talked with you about Jesus...about anything—."

"I wasn't sure what to say. I didn't think you'd believe me." She paused. "There's just so much to say...I've learned so much already...and just for the record, I realize that what you said was true. God didn't kill my parents. I know it was Satan." She sighed, but it was peaceful and she looked up at Don's wall clock.

"I guess I'd better take these down to the cops so they know." Chloe took two steps down. "And in case you were wondering, Heather is at home now, she's fine."

"At home from the hospital?" Don raised his eyebrows.

"I did just like you said, well, like Jesus said in the Bible. I prayed for her and she woke up." Chloe smiled brightly.

"Wow." Wow is right. Don could hardly wrap his brain around that one. Of course God's word was true, but someone was actually woken from a coma? Here is Raile? One of his own students?

"Things are going to change around here, a lot. Really change. I'll see you in school." She made a small wave with her hand and turned away.

Don watched as she walked to her car that was parked at his curb and drove away. The air was

*The Yellow Note*

different just now. Charged with electricity, with hope. Charged with the Holy Spirit. Don knew change would come, just like Chloe said.

"I don't want my dad here with me." James said after Frank informed him of his rights as a minor. Pete had snuck in the interviewing room behind Frank and Brad. And now that he was inside, Frank didn't tell him to leave.

"Why not?" Brad asked.

"He'll just tell me to keep my mouth shut, and I'm tired of keeping my mouth shut. I've kept this secret long enough and I'm done with it." His face was white. He eyed the black garbage bag that was on the other end of the table, the plastic rolled back to view the contents.

"If that's the case go ahead and tell us what you know." Frank told him. He and Brad were sitting at the table with James while Pete stood near the door.

James sighed. "I was with Grace when two of the girls told her that Laura was dead. We were at school. Grace almost passed out and so I brought her home…"

\*      \*      \*

…Grace sobbed uncontrollably as she rode in the front passenger seat of James' vehicle. He felt horrible, but really didn't know what to do for her. He'd always been bad at comforting girls when they cried. Maybe it was because of his military father's strict ways and unemotional life that he was used to.

*The Yellow Note*

James parked in the Hartson's driveway and helped Grace into the house and to her bedroom where she lay on her bed pulling the covers up to her neck as she cried. As she calmed a little, James sat on the edge of her bed and held her hand.

"Do you want me to stay with you?" He asked.

"I'll be fine." She shook her head and dabbed her puffy eyes with the sheet. "I just want to sleep I guess." She gasped a few breaths in.

"Is your mom going to be home soon?"

"No. She works two jobs until eleven tonight."

"I don't really want you to be alone Grace."

Her eyes narrowed a little. "James, lay off. I'll be fine. I just want to cry it out and be left alone."

James nodded and stood up. "I'll come back after football practice okay?" Grace nodded and closed her eyes. James left the house.


Right after the coach let all the guys leave for the night, James hurried to shower and changed and headed straight to Grace's house.

He knocked several times and rung the doorbell, but no one answered. There were lights on...maybe she was still sleeping. But her brother had to be home from school, unless he was at a friends house or something.

James tried the doorknob. It was unlocked. He pushed the door open and stepped inside the small house. "Grace?" He called. The place was a complete disaster with lamps tipped over, broken picture frames, miscellaneous items scattered across the stained carpet. And over by the TV between the side of the sofa and the wall was Zack. He was huddled up so tight, knees to his chest, looking up at James like he'd just seen a horror film.

"Hey Zack." James said. He closed the door behind him. Zack didn't say a word. Something was off. James took a few steps in Zack's direction and saw that he had a bleeding cut on his forehead.

"What happened?" James walked across the living room floor, careful to avoid broken pieces of glass and a pile of dirt that had come from a plant that was ripped from it's pot.

"Grace." Zack whispered. "She went crazy again."

"What?" James offered a hand to help Zack out of his hiding spot but he shook his head no.

"I'll stay here in case she comes out again."

"What do you mean she went crazy again?" James turned to look behind him at Grace's bedroom door. There were no noises or sign of her.

"She does it once in awhile. Like once a month or something. Otherwise she's really fun and nice, but sometimes she just starts screaming and throwing things and breaking everything."

"Why?"

"I don't know." Zack shrugged. "The doctors try and get her to take medicine but sometimes she forgets."

"What's wrong with her?"

"Something in her brain with chemicals. I don't know what they call it. Me and mom just stay out of her way until she calms down and then clean everything up."

*The Yellow Note*

"She beats you up?" James looked closer at the cut on Zack's forehead. It wasn't too bad.

"Yeah." He nodded.

"Is she in her room?"

"Yeah. But I don't know if I'd go in there. Usually we just wait until she comes out herself. Then we know she's fine."

"I think I'll take my chances." James stepped over the mess again and stood in front of Grace's door. He knocked. Nothing. He really just wanted to leave, but he told Grace he'd be over after practice.

"Grace?" He called again. "It's James, I'm coming in okay." He waited a few seconds and then opened the door, excepting to see a wild young woman ready to pounce.

Grace's room looked just like the rest of the house, clothing and other things all over the place. There were holes and dents and scuff marks on her walls that hadn't been there before. And Grace sat on the edge of her bed, hands on her lap as she stared blankly out her window. Her t-shirt and pajama pants were wrinkled and had some blood on them. Probably from her hands that she used to attack the wall.

"Zack told you everything, didn't he?" Grace said in a monotone voice. She kept looking out the window.

"He told me that you had...an issue." James remained by the door. He'd never had to deal with a lunatic before. He really wished that he'd never met Grace now.

"I couldn't help it." She said. "I just hated her. She had you, she had everything and she was so mean

*The Yellow Note*

to everyone. I can't believe how she treated Chloe and Heather, how she just used everyone. Even you, stupid." She glanced up at James with strange eyes. It creeped him out.

What got him even more was what she was implying.

"Did you take your pills today?" He asked, not really thinking, just talking because he was starting to get nervous.

"It doesn't help anyway. Can you do me a favor? I have some bloody clothes over there in my closet." She pointed across the room to James' right. "There's a garbage bag sitting on top of them, I just haven't gotten to it, I've been so tired. Just take the stuff in the garbage bag and burn it somewhere."

Bloody clothes.

James saw the black pants and black long sleeve shirt under the garbage bag, but it didn't register until he saw the black ski mask on top of the pile.

He felt like he might hurl. Or choke. Or pass out. What on earth was she asking him to do? Cover up for her? If he did that he'd get in trouble too. He could go to jail!

"James, just do it." She snapped. "I'm really tired and my hands hurt. And don't get all sorry about it. You hated her too. I suppose since she's dead now I might as well tell you that she wasn't the one who did all that stuff to you, I did it. I spread the rumors and wrecked your things and your car..." She chuckled. "It was fun."

"I can't do this Grace."

*The Yellow Note*

"If you don't, I can prove you were with me when I sent her to darkness." Grace said matter-of-factly. "I had no problem acting devastated this morning now did I? I didn't leave a single print in the house or near it. I didn't leave any hair, any footprints or any other evidence at the Thayer's house. They won't find any books or plans written down anywhere cause I didn't have any. My brother is my alibi and he won't tell. And the only thing that may have been seen is my car. But guess who else has a black, two door sports car?"

Grace waited, a sinister grin spreading across her face.

"Chloe Bennett." She said. "I made sure to park out of the street light so if anyone saw my car last night, they probably won't remember the make or model of the car, much less the license plate number. No one pays attention to those kinds of things."

James stared at the garbage bag.

Grace was a nutcase. If he didn't do what she was telling him to do, he was certain she'd do something to him too. If she'd gone to all the trouble of making it look like Laura was trying to ruin him when it was really her, and now seeing how good of a pretender she could be, Grace could most definitely carry out some evil scheme to end his life as well and make it look like an accident.

Bending down near the closet, James picked up the garbage bag and with the plastic scooped all the bloody clothing into it. They stunk. He felt like retching.

*The Yellow Note*

He tied the bag in a knot and held it away from his legs.

When he looked back up at Grace, she had her eyes closed and was laying down on her bed. James backed up and closed the door on the way out.

Zack was still between the sofa and the wall.

"She tried to get me to get rid of those too." He eyed the bag. "That's why she freaked out, cause I wouldn't do it."

James felt like a pansy.

He should have been able to fend off the deceitful eyes of Miss Grace, but he couldn't. He'd been roped in.

"Are you going to the police?" Zack asked.

"I don't know."

"But you're not going to throw it out like she wants, right?"

"No." James shook his head. "I just don't know what to do yet."

After hearing James finish, the three other men fell silent, deep in thought.

Frank was nodding, taking it all in. Brad had that look that said he'd just about heard it all. Pete was almost in tears. This whole time he'd been wrecked with turmoil, wondering if it could be true that Heather was the killer. And now, hearing both Zack and James' testimony, relief was passing over him.

"Have you and Zack Hartson spoken today?" Frank asked.

"No." James answered, looking confused.

*The Yellow Note*

"Did he ever tell you that he was planning on coming to the cops to tell the truth?"

"The last time I talked to him was that day I took the bag. I've seen him around, but haven't talked to him. He didn't say anything about what he was going to do."

"Okay." Frank nodded again. He looked down at his watch. "Can you sit tight for awhile James?"

"Yeah. I suppose I should call my parents and let them know where I've been." James said.

"You have a cell phone?"

"Yes."

"Go ahead and use that. I'm gonna need you to stay here in this room for awhile." The three men left the room.

In the hallway as they all walked towards the front of the building Frank said, "We'll have Grace in cuffs within the hour."


Pete was told to stay back and wait for Ms. Hartson and the Riley's to either call or show up. Neither did So Pete paced. Back and forth down the hall, passing James and Zack on either side of the room. Zack looked like he was trying to nap, only his foot was jumping wildly on the floor. James had rested his head for awhile on the table, then it appeared as if he were playing games on his cell phone.

At last Pete heard commotion down the hall and then saw little Grace Hartson, face red from crying, being hauled in by two officers who had her by the arms. They led her to the first interviewing room.

*The Yellow Note*

Frank and Brad were right behind her and entered the room too, careful not to let her see down the hall where James and Zack were. Frank pointed to the monitoring room door. Pete scowled. He didn't want to sit behind glass and listen, he wanted to feel the action up close, hear that little brat confess right in front of him.

Pete found a stool behind the one way glass and sat with his arms crossed as Brad questioned Grace.

"...I can't believe you guys arrested me." She said. She didn't seem mad, scared maybe, but not angry.

"You're a suspect Grace, and right now is sure looks like you're more than just that." Brad said. He was trying to stare her down with those intense blue eyes.

"You keep telling me that, but I didn't do anything!" Tears started streaming down her face again. "Laura was my best friend."

"Are you sure you don't want a lawyer Grace?" Frank asked her. He remained near the door like usual.

"I'm not guilty and mom can't afford one anyway." She lifted her cuffed hands up to grab a tissue on the table.

"The state can pay for a lawyer."

"I don't need one. I'm not guilty."

"Don't forget you're being recorded." Brad told her. She nodded and blew her nose.

"I know." She said.

"Where were you when Laura was murdered?"

*The Yellow Note*

"I was with my brother." She sniffed. "We were watching movies all night, I even called Laura to ask her if she wanted to come over. I think I called three times. She never answered."

"Did you leave the house at all that night?"

"After Laura didn't return my calls, I left to go see if she was at home. I got halfway there and realized I had all the party supplies in my car. If she saw them the surprise would be off, so I came home."

"A witness saw a black sports car parked a few blocks from Laura's house that night. Your car fits the description."

Grace frowned. "I don't know what else to say, I wasn't in her house at all that day." Her eyes didn't twitch or steer from Brad's at all. She was so convincing. If Pete didn't know better, he'd believe her.

"So if we talked to your brother he'd be saying the same thing." Brad said.

"Yes." She nodded and wiped her nose again. "But, there is something."

Brad waited.

Pete got closer to the window.

"I saw Chloe Bennett when I drove by, before I realized that I didn't want Laura to see the party supplies. Chloe's car was parked a few blocks away from Laura's."

"Did you see Chloe or just the car?"

"I saw movement in the car, I couldn't tell if it was her or not."

"Why didn't you say something before, when you were questioned the first time?"

*The Yellow Note*

Grace glanced over at Frank, then at the window where Pete was. He knew she couldn't see him but he felt like she could. "I didn't want to be a tattle tail.

"Just a minute ago you said you got half way to Laura's and then turned around cause of the party stuff in your car..

Grace blinked.

"Maybe this is all just made up and you thought you had your bases covered but now you don't know what to say." Brad said, he leaned in closer to her over the table.

"I didn't kill her." Her eyes narrowed.

"It was you parked a few streets from Laura's, wasn't it Grace? All this time you were planning to kill Laura because you couldn't have what she had... a nice house, a fancy car, all the money she wanted, a football star boyfriend..."

Grace's breathing changed.

"It was you, wasn't it Grace?" Brad probed more. Then, without warning, Grace jumped out of her seat, her chair flying behind her wildly. Brad stood up and backed away. Frank put his hand on his gun at his hip.

"Fine!" Grace screamed. "It was me! I did it! I thought I was doing the whole school a favor by getting rid of the most horrid person ever! All she did was hate everyone. She was mean to those gothic girls all the time, back stabbed all of her so-called friends...who knows what she said about me. So big deal, big frickin' deal! A crazy brat is dead. One less jerk to put up with!" Her fists were clenched tight in front of her, bound by those cuffs.

*The Yellow Note*

"How did you get into Laura's house Grace?" Brad asked.

"The code, duh." She rolled her eyes. "I'm not stupid. I watched her punch it in so many times I had it memorized."

Pete sat wide eyed, careful not to miss a thing. Brad just sat and waited. Grace took the opportunity to spill it all.

"Was Laura already dead when you called her cell phone three times that night?"

"I had to make things look right...kept you guys off my trail in the first place didn't it?" She paused.

"I waited for a chance to find a scapegoat, actually I found three. I wrecked a bunch of James' stuff and spread rumors about him and made it look like Laura did it. And since Heather and Chloe made it plain that they didn't care for me either, and I knew they hated Laura, I decided they'd be perfect. I didn't have to wait long."

"And how did you do that?" Brad asked. He stayed close to the wall. Pete noticed two officers standing outside the door, waiting to come in when needed.

"I'm sure you found the blue water bottle. I know about forensics, not that hard to cover things...be careful...take your time...Heather was drinking from it one day during our lunch break. Her prints were all over it. She threw it away. When they were long gone I used a napkin to get the bottle, making sure I didn't wreck the prints. So I planted it."

Pete stood up and pressed his head against the glass.

*The Yellow Note*

*That little witch!*

He wanted to jump through the window and strangle that little maniac! If she wouldn't have used that bottle to try and incriminate Heather, she wouldn't be in the hospital now

"Everyone should be glad I put them all out of misery." Grace said.

"Do you realize you just confessed to murder, Grace?"

"Of course I do, you idiot!" She yelled. "But it doesn't matter. The judge will find me not guilty. Once everyone sees how cruel Laura was, they'll wish they were the hero that saved the day."

As Grace was talking, Frank let the officers in and they escorted her out of the room. Pete could hear her shouting things as they dragged her down the hallway and to the booking area.

Brad turned to the window where Pete stood and a huge smile crept up onto his face. "Good thing you're not a betting man or you'd have been out some cash."

\*     \*     \*

Pete walked down the hall, passing James' parents and Frank as they came to see their son. And when he got to the lobby Ms. Hartson came busting in, smelling like smoke. Pete pointed her in the right direction to find Zack and she hurried away.

And now Pete was alone in the front entry, only the sound of the receptionist coughing every now and then. He didn't really know what to do now. His knees were weak, his heart was pounding...it was almost as

*The Yellow Note*

if the constant pounding was actually words...*Time to change, time to change, time to change.*

He couldn't go home to that unbearably quiet house with a son who kept to his room and a wife that hardly knew he existed. But the pounding of the heart continued, the words echoing through his brain.

As he walked slowly, staring at the floor, Pete was unaware that the front door was opening.

"Mr. Monson?" A female voice. Pete looked up. It was Chloe Bennett. Anger rose up instantly within him...but now there was no reason to be mad at her, she was innocent...at least of murder.

"Can I talk to you about some things that involve Laura?" She asked.

"Um...actually, no. I'm not on the case any more."

"Oh." Her face fell to her hands that held some pieces of white paper. "Who can I talk to then?"

"Frank or Brad. Just take the hall on the left and walk in, an officer is down there, he'll be able to show you where."

She nodded. "Okay, thanks." She hesitated, then started to walk off but stopped and turned towards him again. "You should probably go home, I think you'll want to talk to your family." Chloe smiled a little and then walked off down the hall, leaving Pete alone again.

*Why did she say that? Why should I listen to that girl?*

But Pete realized that he really didn't have anywhere to go and it was getting late. And more

*The Yellow Note*

than anything now he wanted to see his wife and kids and make things right.

Inside the house Pete took his shoes off on the little mat next to the wall, threw his keys down on the entry table and noticed the light was on in the living room. Probably Steve...Kristine would be downstairs if she were watching TV. But he didn't hear the television. Curious, Pete walked through the front hall and stopped dead in his tracks as he saw who was sitting there.

Heather.

The sight of his first born back from the dark comatose state made tears well up in his eyes. His knees felt weak. Was this real?

"Hi dad." She looked up from a cup of tea she had in her hand and smiled wide at him.

"Heather..." It came out as a whisper and he wept. And he rushed to her and threw his arms around her. The tea spilled on the carpet and the mug dropped to the floor, but neither of them cared. He sobbed on her shoulder for a good long time, until he felt someone else's presence in the room.

Pete wiped his eyes and looked up. Kristine was sitting next to them, eyes watery. Steve was just a face full of grin as he stood behind the sofa.

"Didn't you get my messages?" Kristine asked softly.

"No...I mean, I knew my phone was ringing...I didn't want to talk. Oh God." Pete let his head hang in sorrow. "I can't believe how awful I've been. I can't stand myself…all this time and I've forgotten God…I've forgotten Jesus."

Pete rested his head on Heather's knee and cried more, apologizing to his family and to God for being a poor husband, father and horrible example of Christ. Together, all of them vowed to change things. Most of all, they all knew they needed to return to what was most important. Jesus.

"What happened?" Pete asked after what seemed like an eternity of crying and hugging and apologies.

"Chloe prayed for me." Heather said. "She got saved dad. Mr. Graham was the one that made her think. She read the Bible and she just believed it. She believed it so much that she came to pray for me in the hospital. And now, here I am." She gleamed. "I'm alive, I feel good…a little weak, but getting stronger and it's all because Chloe just changed her heart and believed."

Suddenly, everything all came flooding to Pete, as if he had new eyes. As if scales and calluses had fallen from him. The investigation, all the sleepless nights, the lack of clues and so much confusion and frustration. And Heather. All hell had seemed to break loose at once…and now…now in just a matter of hours it seemed the windows of Heaven had opened causing the truth to be revealed, puzzle pieces fitting where they should and in the midst of it all, a massive miracle had taken place with his own daughter.

"I feel so bad now…" He said. "I treated Chloe so badly. I didn't even give her a chance…if I had been a better Christian, and shown her Jesus.

*The Yellow Note*

Pete stood up slowly, wiping his cheeks with the back of his hand.

"I have to go do something." He said. They all looked at him with curious faces. "I have to talk to Chloe. I'll be back as soon as I can." He walked through the living room and as he came to the door, he turned to look back at his family. They were huddled up on the sofa, watching him. They had new eyes too, he could feel it and it made him smile.

This was a good day.

A very good day.

# EPILOGUE

In the months following Heather's awaking and Chloe's change of heart, things in both families were turned upside down.

Chloe and her sister Mara began working on a solid sisterly relationship, praying together, keeping each other strong and finding peace without their loving parents.

The once distant and dysfunctional Monson family finally found restoration and came together as a family should. Pete and Kristine found the love of their youth and sought to keep the bond of the family tight. Both of them took more time off of work to spend with each other and the children.

Don Graham soon found that keeping a perfect, orderly routine was no longer possible. Morning prayer at the high school had started and the students were using his classroom for a meeting place. At least a few nights a week a group of students would show up at his house, wanting to pray or seeking help for one of their friends. Brownie liked all the new attention and Don was getting used to breaking out of his

*The Yellow Note*

mold. Of course, the principal was keeping a close eye on him, but Don knew it was all in God's hands.

Grace Hartson was tried as an adult because of the nature of the crime she committed and was shortly thereafter sentenced to a state prison for the mentally insane. Her brother Zack soon started attending church with the Monson family and eventually gave his life to Jesus. Ms. Hartson was soon to follow.

James Riley quit all the sports he was involved in and stopped going to school until a recently converted atheist befriended him and encouraged him to come to the student prayer Wednesday mornings. It didn't take long before James saw the reality of Christ and it changed his life.

Detective Brad Cohan watched in amazement as the world around him changed, Pete was constantly working on him in a loving way, encouraging him to seek for truth. And Brad was indeed on the quest for what life was all about. Pete knew someday he'd find it...he just hoped he was there when it happened.

Raile, in itself, had begun to see a spark of change. Church attendance was on a rise, hospital patients were on the decline, thanks to teams of bold young adults who were spreading the Word of God wherever they went. Bars were losing customers, porn shops and strip joints were going out of business. Crime was at its lowest point in years.

And little by, the spark was catching on. Neighboring cities were seeing change...even the nation...but that's another story.

# A NOTE FROM THE AUTHOR

Do you know where you are going when you die?

Is your life full, do you enjoy living, or are you depressed, confused, afraid or just plain unsatisfied with your life?

Jesus came and died, not only for the forgiveness of our sins, but so that we could have an abundant life full of peace, joy and security. The Bible says in Romans 10:9-10 that if a person confesses with their mouth and believes in their heart that Jesus is Lord and that God raised him from the dead you will be saved.

Saved from what, you may ask. Saved from eternal separation from God, saved from the fears and torments of the soul that keep you from enjoying life. Contrary to what many believe, God is a god of love, not hate. He doesn't want to strike you dead with lightning because you sin, or give you cancer if you do something wrong to your neighbor. That is the devil, Satan, who does those things.

*The Yellow Note*

God wants to restore your life to what He intended it to be before the fall of mankind in the Garden of Eden. He wants you to have peace, happiness, security, love, prosperity and all other good things. The Father God is not a task master. The Bible is not a set of rules, it's a road map to freedom. God did not tell you that you shouldn't be a drunkard or adulterer or any other sinful thing just to control you. If He wanted to control us, He just would. He's God, He has the power to do that, but He won't. He wants you to be free. He wants you to love him back of your own free will, otherwise it wouldn't be love and we'd all be robots.

The reason God put guidelines in the Bible is for our own benefit. If we drink it hurts us. It damages our kidneys and livers and when taken to the extreme could kill us. If we commit adultery it causes problems in marriages and destroys families because of the emotional distress. If we lie it breaks trust people have in us when they find out we lied to them. As with any sin, the effects happen in us, maybe not right away, but eventually, it will come back to us.

Are you a parent? Have you ever fallen in love? Think about a family member whom you love deeply. This is how God feels about us. He loves us so much that He sent Jesus to die. He allowed His own Son to be killed on the cross so that we wouldn't be separated from Him anymore. He doesn't despise us, he wants us, and He cherishes us. His love is so deep, so wide, so full, that it hurts him when we hurt, it pains him when we walk away from Him and don't listen to Him. He just wants to be with us.

*The Yellow Note*

Salvation is not just to keep you out of Hell. It means a complete saving. Healing from disease or pain or anything that is wrong with your body. Put your trust in Jesus and He will heal your body, He will change your life and turn your sadness to joy, your fears into security.

There is no formula to get saved or as the Bible calls it, born again. It's simple. You must believe that Jesus was the only Son of God, that He died on the cross and God raised Him from the dead. The Bible says that anyone who calls on the name of the Lord will be saved. Just call out to Him, ask Him to save you from eternal death and from any other thing that you need help with. He will hear you and answer you.

Before we were born, God put inside of each one of us gifts and talents unique to only us. Maybe you know what some of them are already. I encourage you to continue to use those gifts and talents the way God intended, pray and ask Him to help you understand how to use them more efficiently.

Maybe you think you don't have any, let me assure you, you do. What God has gifted you with may not be so visible as with other things. Perhaps you have a knack for business, or for gardening, or painting...or it could be that you like to spend time with people and help them, or give them things. Just because it may look on the outside like you have nothing to offer, look again. Ask God to reveal it to you and keep trying things. You never know what you like or what you're good at until you try.

I hope to see you some day in Heaven.

Printed in the United States
207238BV00001B/109-315/P